ManBug

ManBug

George K. Ilsley

Arsenal Pulp Press
Vancouver

ARSENAL PULP PRESS
Suite 200 – 341 Water Street
Vancouver, BC
Canada V6B 1B8
arsenalpulp.com

The publisher gratefully acknowledges the support of the Canada Council for the Arts and the British Columbia Arts Council for its publishing program, and the Government of Canada through the Book Publishing Industry Development Program for its publishing activities.

Editing by Brian Lam
Text and cover design by Shyla Seller
Front cover photograph by Odelia Cohen, back cover photograph by Stefan Klein

This is a work of fiction. Any resemblance of characters to persons either living or deceased is purely coincidental.

A section of *Manbug* previously appeared as "Clamp and Groove" in *Quickies 3,* edited by James C. Johnstone (Arsenal Pulp Press, 2003).

Printed and bound in Canada

Library and Archives Canada Cataloguing in Publication

Ilsley, George K., 1958-
    ManBug / George K. Ilsley.

ISBN 1-55152-203-9

    I. Title. II. Title: Man bug.

PS8567.L74M35 2006   C813'.6   C2006-900334-3

ISBN-13 978-1-55152-203-6

*This book is dedicated to Dorje Tröllo,
the Crazy Wisdom form of Padmasambhava,
the father and protector of all beings.*

Part 1

SEBASTIAN EXPLAINS EVERYTHING

It takes little talent to see clearly
what lies under one's nose, a good
deal of it to know in which direction
to point that organ.

– W.H. Auden, from "Writing" in
The Dyer's Hand, and Other Essays

just start somewhere

Sebastian was born in a root cellar on a warm October evening. It was cool in there. It was always cool in there. The dirt floor felt alive under his sprawling fingertips, as he waited to become.

Metamorphosis was a constant theme for Sebastian, just as impermanence was for Tom. That is another difference they had in common.

There is a whole host of differences between Tom and Sebastian, if a person wanted to list them.

Tom, for example, was born into a weird hippie commune, and Tom is not even his real name, which is long and Sanskrit and is not to be used. Tom is the name he adopted when he left the weird hippie commune to become as one with the world of men.

Metamorphosis.

Impermanence.

Over and over again.

Sebastian's first friends were the many-legged.

Tom spent his early years sleeping on the children's platform with an ever-changing assortment of waifs with big, unruly hair. The children were expected to get along, and to some extent, take care of each other.

And they did.

Sebastian would watch a mosquito swell dark red on his own blood, and try not to disturb its meal.

It was cool in the root cellar, and smelled of clean dirt, and sometimes Sebastian imagines he is still there in his perfect little hideaway, with the many-legged, and the packed earth alive under his fingertips.

His first friends had no voice, and so now, he must speak up.

on the meaning of impermanence and metamorphosis

Sebastian used to have a job.

Sebastian used to be a research entomologist.

Mostly, Sebastian researched the development of pesticides.

Much about this work in the killing field disturbed Sebastian (for example, the casual use of the concept "termination opportunity").

When distressed, Sebastian tended to express conflict. A blurt of truth might escape his lips before he could help himself. This could be, for example, while compiling mortality data, or tweaking a statistical analysis of residual contamination by increasing the sample size. Smoothing the result, it was called. Smoothing the rough edges of truth: the research facility, through a shift in perspective, became a factory generating statistics. They virtually manufactured data, based on demand.

Statisticians called the data massage "increasing the sample size."

Managers called it "broadening the research horizon."

Sebastian called it "diluting the evidence." Diluting

it until the answer came back, "no detectable residue."
Just like sausage from Chernobyl. Diluted until no
longer considered radioactive.

But all the poison was still in there.

Somewhere. Somebody was eating it.

Sebastian was laid off.

Well, not exactly.

His contract was not extended.

True, but not really.

He feels laid off. They told him not to come back.

Might as well be laid off.

There was a spill at a test site. They were researching
a promising neurotoxin, a potent carcinogen which (in
the shorter term) was remarkably effective even in trace
amounts for wiping out nervous systems. The focus of
their research was the dispersal of this neurotoxin to
target bugs, and eventually, hopefully, the right bugs.

No other research was mandated. Through
a reprieve from the laws of science, spraying this
poison over crops was seen to have few environmental
consequences worth investigating. Collateral damage
all around the food chain? No alarm bells went off.
Horribly toxic, yes, if used as directed, but otherwise
posed no risk.

This was the heyday of pesticides, when no problem couldn't be fixed by dumping enough poison on it.[1]

Sebastian may have been stubborn. He may have persisted with an unpopular line of reasoning. He didn't intend to be off-putting, but sometimes he had that effect. Sebastian as always was just trying to be reasonable and logical. And patient, because it was very frustrating to see science subverted by elements of faith.

Science is supposed to be based on solid research, logic, and reason. But if a chemical company is funding the research, obviously it is reasonable to place one's greatest faith in chemicals: there was logic in that.

And that is the circular science of rationalization.

Anyway, there was an unexpected spill (which became known at the lab as the "premature evacuation") during the mortality assessment / community penetration / environmental dispersal trials. One immediate side effect of exposure to this neurotoxin was confusion.

Sebastian presented investigators with convincing symptoms (although it took him a while to figure out what had happened).

The symptoms persisted; tests suggested a metabolic signature of the neurotoxin, while other investigations were inconclusive. Sebastian was placed on long-term disability. Told to stay home. Told, specifically, not to come into his prior place of

---

[1] We are still in this heyday.

employment without being invited in writing.

He was not laid off, and his contract was not extended.

He was not supposed to go in to work.

He was not working there anymore.

It was not known what Sebastian was going to do.

That is a lot of nots.

Sebastian has time on his hands and is using this time (and his hands) to make a permanent record of a number of transitory things.

twisted three times

He almost took his mother's life. The water broke hours and hours before, but he was wedged in tight and twisted and refused to budge. For a time, the doctor feared the worst. The doctor took his father aside and said, "There's nothing we can do for the child. But your wife might pull through." Might.

The cord was wrapped three times around his neck and his head was blue. Jolted from his liquid dream, torn from a silken sac and startled awake, he burst out howling and pretty much cried the next several months. They worried about brain damage. Remember, his head was blue.

That's just one explanation why Sebastian turned out like he did. Why else would he spend so much time in the root cellar? There had to be a reason.

Another theory is that his father was never there. Or, blame his mother, because she was. She babied him. He was wedged tight in her heart: they were maybe too close. Everyone was glad when Sebastian moved away, although his mother missed him desperately. He still talked to her all the time, in his head and on the phone.

When Sebastian hears certain words, he sees colours. The word "deciduous" is like a wash of green.

The word "mother" used to spark bright yellow, but now has faded to a kind of background beige.

Sebastian doesn't know what this means, but assumes it is normal.

the order of concerns

Tom carries within him both structure and chaos, the
two counterbalanced.

In the sense that every action has an equal and opposite
reaction, this counterbalance of structure and chaos
ends up attracting Sebastian.

It is this paradox of balance which simultaneously
makes Tom appear complete, perplexing, and attractive.
And enormously frustrating.

Sebastian, it has been said, is overly concerned with
order, and categories, and naming. It has been said
that Sebastian is doggedly humourless in his pursuit
of the meanings and boundaries of masculinity. It is
to be hoped that through the study of Tom, many of
Sebastian's questions about maleness may now be more
fully addressed.

freak show

School was the worst.
 School was where Sebastian felt most like a freak.

Sebastian, along with so many others, was a geek before geek was chic.
 Also at that point in the history of the development of human culture, it must be acknowledged, frankly, that "gay geeks" were yet to be identified as a niche market.
 Sebastian was ahead of the geek chic curve, and ahead of the gay geek curve, and to this day, has never even heard of a gay geek chic curve, or square, or whatever form such a thing would take.
 In his own personal freak show, Sebastian was doing gay geek chic before anyone had even heard of such a thing. Sebastian was part of an important minor trend in human development in his own lifetime, without even knowing it at the time.
 At the time, at school it was best to be ignored. That was best.
 But that did not always happen.

knowing what you have done

Sebastian knows that if you love something too much, you kill it.

He learned that the hard way.

If you could not leave it alone, not even for a second, you took its life.

He has already loved too much. He had to learn, hands off.

That was a long time ago.

Sebastian wonders if he would recognize the symptoms if he loved Tom too much. Some indications are there. He certainly was not "hands off."

And in his thoughts, he did not leave Tom alone. Not even for a second.

golden parachute

Sebastian imagined his golden parachute holding him aloft, floating him along like a spider's sail, until drifting down to a new place.

A different place.

Hopefully, the right place.

The golden parachute was only part of this picture. The golden parachute carried him aloft, but at the other end of the journey, there was the need to arrive.

It was an act of faith, an expression of complete and utter powerlessness, for the spider to launch a sail into the face of the wind and say take me, take me there, take me to the new better world.

Sebastian had trouble visualizing what the right place for him would be right now. The golden parachute if anything provided too much buoyancy. There was too much freedom and not enough necessity.

He knows this is just a phase: before metamorphosis.

He does not know what this metamorphosis might involve, and the convergence of the unpredictable is startling. He cannot do anything without thinking about it, and he cannot think about what is unpredictable. Or else he thinks about it too much. The need for complete metamorphosis paralyzes, like a poison. And the need to avoid incomplete metamorphosis can be crippling.

Sebastian did what he could to extend the life of the parachute, so he wouldn't have to think beyond it. He jettisoned. He sold his car, cancelled the cable, cut to the bone, as they say, and let himself go. He floated. Sebastian went with the feeling that he could just coast from here.

He was powerless, and adrift.

And maybe confused.

For all of Tom's flakiness and his legendary willy-wallowing, Tom was also someone who knew how to reach out to someone who has stumbled.

This period of collapse in Sebastian's life was actually what cemented his relationship with Tom. Turmoil as the foundation for stability: Sebastian could not have predicted this, and yet there it was, something for him to think about.

When Sebastian was set adrift in his golden parachute and his spirits soared in the opposite direction, Tom suddenly became very interested in Sebastian. Tom kept calling, ignoring normal phone call trading rules and phoning Sebastian several times in a row. And when Tom reached Sebastian, he would sound grateful, not annoyed or frustrated. Not demanding.

Tom was being so damn nice.

Only later did Sebastian wonder, was the mortar of Tom's niceness composed of kindness, or recruitment?

the age of specialists

Sebastian's brain used to focus almost entirely on Sebastian and matters directly related to his own care and feeding.

Now he thinks about Tom so much it is like his brain has been rewired.

Being in love is not easily distinguishable from what it must be like to be totally taken over by an alien life form.

Sebastian wonders, does the orb web spider think, "Is this what love means?" when taken over by a parasitic wasp?[2]

The stories Sebastian most wants to share are amazing true stories from a land of everyday miracles.

The miraculousness of these everyday miracles

---

[2] It is highly unlikely a spider's thoughts are anywhere near so whimsical. Structured, yes. But not whimsical.

never fails to stun. Often, people are so overwhelmed they are totally unable to react when they hear amazing true stories about insects.

Yet so much is unknown about the everyday miracles. This is distancing, to the average listener.

Sebastian, for example, wants to tell the parable of the parasitic wasp. He wants to tell the whole story, but so much that is unknown is already on full display. The unknown is taking up all the space in the story.

The parasitic wasp takes over the spider; the spider's own programming is interrupted and the wasp's program intervenes and dominates.

How is this done?

We do not know.

How does the wasp manage to insert its own subroutines while leaving the spider's life support systems intact?

We do not know.

The spider still lives, but now it serves the wishes of its parasitic master, spinning a cocoon for its own metamorphosis into the sacrificial host. Take, eat, this is my body.

How does the parasitic wasp accomplish all this?

We do not know.

When so much is unknown, the story is missing much of its substance. There are elements and themes, there is life and death, but what is really happening?

The shrouded spider becomes a nest of wasps: how did such an extreme specialization ever evolve?

No one has a clue.

Sebastian was confused long before any spill at a test site.

initial phase

They had been dating. That is, seeing each other.
Somewhere between fuck buddies and boyfriends (these
are labels Sebastian does not completely understand).
Usually having a lot of sex, when they did get together.

That was the thing with Tom. He was very sexual.
And so his experience of the world turned out to be
sexual. Tom's talent is then to be constantly surprised,
wow, everyone's so sexual.

As if he hadn't been involved in creating this all
along.

So too with Sebastian, the Tom experience was very
sexual during this initial phase. Before they started
living together.

During the initial phase, Sebastian tried not to
think about Tom's sexuality. Whatever he encountered
went past quickly and left few traces. Sebastian saw
Tom's sexuality as a blur, a whirl, flurries of activities
and acting out. Sebastian could not have guessed Tom's
intentions, so he tried not to speculate. His motto was,
don't ask. In fact, neither of them looked too closely.

Sex for Sebastian has never been something to get all that carried away with. Sex was a pool Sebastian dipped his toe in, sometimes more than his toe, until withdrawing again, back to dry land. The pursuit of sex, when he thought about it, was something like a hobby, which of course he enjoyed, but mostly kept tucked away in a drawer because he just didn't have time for it.

Tom carried with him a concentration of excitement, and when Sebastian moved closer, everything became a blur, but in a good way. This concentration is perhaps what other people call sexy. Sebastian was over-stimulated, by Tom's eyes, by his smell, but did not freak out. Tom's eyes were too much and he smelled like more, but somehow Tom carried with him the possibility of so much excitement that there was space for Sebastian as well.

Things happened in their excitement, things that are a little blurry now – the exact sequence of moves and how what happened happened, and why right then and not forty-five minutes later. In the heat of excitement, laughter was a purple blur, and this warm purple washed over Sebastian's face and kissed his furrowed brow. Time passed quickly.

Something within that splash and blur changed Sebastian.

That was the initial phase.

Tom's independent accidental discovery

"Manbug" is a term every student of entomology discovers, in a spontaneous playful moment, generally upon viewing ladybugs in a slightly sexualized context: "Male ladybug? Shouldn't that be *man*bug?" The student of entomology then laughs at this joke, but never repeats it.

The observation holds that every entomologist (even amateurs) will make the manbug joke once, provoked perhaps by the sight of ladybugs humping like ridiculous little tortoises: "One must be a manbug, hardy har har."

Tom had never heard the mandatory manbug joke. Manbug was Tom's independent accidental discovery.

Tom started out somewhere else entirely, then through a twisted backwards route, arrived at manbug in that manner.

Tom started with Bugman, which was to be an ironic superhero nickname for Sebastian. Tom feels people would be better able to express important elements of being through identities signified by ironic superhero nicknames,[3] but when he opened his mouth to say *Bugman*, out came Manbug. Which is an even better nickname, apparently.

Tom says Manbug has nothing to do with ladybugs, and so, officially, that is how Manbug became Sebastian's nickname. Tom gave it to him, accidentally.

An accidental gift of dyslexia.

Not all gifts are accidents, but this one was.

Accidents are gifts, Tom says. And he should know.

---

[3] It is appropriate that some of these superhero nicknames remain secret.

what they say about Sebastian

They say Sebastian has no sense of humour. But that is simply not true.

Why, just last week he told a funny story in a social setting.

No one laughed, but still it shows that Sebastian has a sense of humour.

෴

They say that Sebastian cannot understand what goes on around him. Half the time when he asks, "Hey, what's going on?" no one else seems to know.

෴

They say he is "impervious to social cues."

"That's me, Mister Impervious," he said to Tom.

Tom said, "Mister Impervious can be your nickname. It does have perv" – Tom's strong hands, touched with grace – "right here in the middle. Feeling impervious, are we? Mister?"

෴

They say Sebastian has a one-track mind, and he
wonders, how else does anything ever get done?

They say he always talks about Tom now, that
everything he talks about always comes back to Tom.
That Sebastian is so impervious he can't even open his
mouth without Tom immediately crossing his lips.

There is nothing really to say about any of this, except
that Tom has become his own category, and that means
there is a place for him. So he is always there, like a
screensaver in Sebastian's universe, and it is okay if
Sebastian talks about him.
    The same people who roll their eyes at Sebastian's
"obsession" are always eager, instead, to talk talk talk
about their own small boring lives.

And they say Sebastian is not aware of stuff that goes
on around him.

insect autopsies

Some hung straight down with their heads full of snot. The snot was usually black or brown slime.

Other cadavers were withered and dry, attached at both shriveled ends.

Sebastian had one so-called entomology contract performing instant autopsies on gypsy moth larvae. The work was interesting for the first few minutes and consistently tedious after that. There was a lot of public money being directed towards gypsy moth control programs, and so the point of this research was to spend even more money to supposedly determine what actually was killing gypsy moth larvae.

The cause of death was to be decided in a glance. A two-second autopsy on each of thousands of gypsy moth larvae, and designating a cause of death: bacteria, fungus, parasite, environmental toxin. Or, the box never to be ticked because it defeated the whole purpose of research: Unknown. Sebastian was encouraged (instructed) to, yes, just guess, rather than attribute any death to Unknown. Or else what was the point of research?

Sebastian twitched, restraining his answer: "The point of research is to learn, not to guess?" The point was, Sebastian wanted that job, so he went along with what he was told to do. He guessed.

The feature of note in insect autopsies was cadaver persistence. Cadaver persistence was by far the most helpful indicator. The soft, moist bags of dark-brown snot degenerated rapidly, and so were mercifully rare. The heads-down dangling little slime bags did not last. The shriveled husks did.

The main feature of these dry husks, mummified by a killer fungus, was cadaver persistence. That cadaver had become a fruiting body. And life went on. Or death. Whichever it was.

Sebastian's shadow fell over the tray of cadavers as he leaned in for the count.

Sebastian's entire research project was wiped out almost overnight when a mysterious new fungus appeared out of nowhere and eliminated every gypsy moth larva within hundreds of miles. There were no gypsy moth larvae left to attempt to kill with experimental poisons.

Funds then flowed like magic to researchers seeking to genetically engineer a mysterious lethal fungus for speed and efficacy.

Sebastian hoped that no super killer fungus developed a taste for mammals. Otherwise, fruiting bodies will blanket the planet.

pet history

Before Tom, Sebastian had a pet turtle.

That is collapsing things a bit. Sebastian was very young when he had a pet turtle. The turtle was his first real pet, since apparently an ant colony does not count. The turtle was supposed to encourage Sebastian to be more sociable.

Obviously, his parents struggled with deficits of their own. What were they thinking?[4] Perhaps a kitten

---

[4] Since Sebastian was only interested in insects, it was felt that a reptile might be a step in the right direction: towards so-called higher life forms. Also, the turtle was vegetarian. Other possible reptile companions ate worms and insects, which seemed problematic (i.e., could easily become a worm/insect factory). A tarantula would have been perfect, but was not even considered due to issues of prejudice against spiders and other arthropods. Sebastian would have so loved a pink-toed tarantula. To this day, he sees shivers of red at the thought of the forlorn yet whimsical chirp of a cricket, growing ever fainter, its insides partially liquified and predigested by the venomous bite of a large hairy spider. Having the life slowly sucked out of it while it rubbed its forewings together. Each chirp a weaker crimson. That is the sweet cry of nature, and taught Sebastian a great deal about life when he first glimpsed it fade fade fade away.

or a puppy would be nice, something furry and warm. No. Sebastian's parents got him a pet that was cold-blooded and slow and lived in a shell.

There was a process to follow in selecting a pet for Sebastian. Sebastian was consulted but ignored. Tarantulas were ruled out. Imperial scorpions were ruled out. Incredibly, even pseudo-scorpions were ruled out, just because they looked like scorpions.

A decision was finally made, and Sebastian was given a turtle. A very nice turtle as turtles go, but nowhere near as extraordinary as ants. He named it Salmonella, which looking back was rather campy for someone so young and supposedly socially retarded.

The giving of the name, unfortunately, represented the peak of his interest in the turtle. The turtle had absolutely no organizational achievements and offered little companionship. The ants, at least, were watchable as a pattern of functioning chaos, but their destiny had been revisited. The ants were banished because there were other ants in the house, even though the other ants in the house had nothing whatsoever to do with Sebastian's ants. They were not the same ants at all. There was no connection between Sebastian's ants and the other ants in the house, but even so, Sebastian had to give up his ants, which was not fair, and given a stupid turtle who could, at most, eat lettuce and doze.

Salmonella died during a heat wave, evidently from the complications of apathy.

And Sebastian did not care.

Obviously, that was a very long time ago. Things have changed a lot since then.

kinship

Even though he was not related to them, and even though as a child it was nowhere near clear what Sebastian would become, Sebastian does feel some kinship with those first four autistic children identified by Dr. Asperger as possessing sufficiently distinguishing characteristics to be considered "high-functioning" (and therefore possibly valuable: Do Not Exterminate).

Vienna, late 1930s, early 1940s: in the maw of the Nazi extermination machine, a diagnosis of Asperger's syndrome was meant to save the life of the child so labelled. From a group of "special needs" children classed as mental defectives and being sent to their death, Dr. Asperger selected four individuals who were to live. These differently gifted children were the basis for Dr. Asperger's research, and the first examples of what became known as Asperger's syndrome.

Asperger's syndrome is used now to describe people who, basically, are weird and smart in some ways (like computer programming), but have undeveloped social skills and little emotional intelligence or empathy. Of course, this leaves immense room for individual variation within the syndrome, and within the broader autistic spectrum. Naturally enough, Dr. Asperger himself is said to have displayed many traits characteristic of Asperger's syndrome.

"High-functioning" was not a phrase teachers automatically reached for when they thought of Sebastian. He rocked, he moaned, he phased in and out, and wrapped his arms around his head. He did what he wanted and sometimes he wanted to shut out stimulation. Sebastian knew people by their smell, and this before any child wore a fragrance other than their very own. Sebastian could smell each person's ambient aroma, their cocoon of toothpaste and green-apple shampoo, their horse named Shadow, their rushed hygiene and grease-monkey aspirations. The forbidden cigarettes and camouflage cough-drops. He could smell what they had for breakfast. He would not even look at people, just smell them as they passed by a few feet away, and he would know too much for his own good.

The preference was that he just not speak ever, so mostly he didn't. Sebastian developed his own interests, becoming obsessed with nonsense, such as naming the colours of fear and the inexpressible meaning of meaning. After he became captivated by insects, he spoke of nothing else for years. People begged for some simple rocking to and fro instead of all the bug talk.

It was a struggle to keep Sebastian in the normal school system, where he did poorly, and it was only a complete lack of community resources which kept him there. Bugboy did not blossom in school. He was easily upset. He rocked and phased and buried his head in his arms. Kids noticed him only to tease him. Sebastian hid. He hid from the names and the bruises and from the walls with no doors he always ended up facing, when given a time out. He hid and hid and hid.

He hid inside Bugboy.

Sebastian was not related to these first four children recognized by Dr. Hans Asperger, a Viennese pediatrician. But these young frontrunners, dubbed "little professors" because of their oblivious indulgence in pedantic obsessions, may have saved Sebastian's life.

Like an ancestor, these differently gifted children who were not to be exterminated made Sebastian's life possible.

Otherwise, a child like Sebastian could have been born into a world where he was squashed like a bug before he even had a chance to fully develop into the man he has become.

Manbug, Tom says. That is what Sebastian has become.

A big crusty Manbug.

clamp and groove

Tom and Sebastian first met in the shade of an oak tree at the edge of the reception. Confusion helped bring them together.

"The future," Sebastian had said, "is insects."

But what Tom heard was, "The future is sex," and he was provoked.

Tom glowed at the news. The future is sex.

And Sebastian felt so good for once, having but stated the obvious and receiving such a positive response.

Sebastian had put off talking about entomology as long as he could. But then Tom somehow managed to mention being a dyslexic bisexual.

Sebastian felt twisted out of position by this information, and by Tom's warm brown eyes fringed with lashes so black, so lush, they looked air-brushed. Momentarily stunned, Sebastian just blurted out, "You know, in so many ways, the future is insects." There it was out in the open, and he saw the gleam in Tom's eyes, and Tom's big goofy grin. Sebastian felt welcome. It was all very green.

And so, having fallen silent on the topic, Sebastian

lured Tom home and before the kettle had boiled they were looking at large glossy pictures.

"These aren't true bugs," Sebastian was quick to point out. "True bugs are another family. I'll show you those later."

Tom noted the books, the photos, the fascination, the large poster of a praying mantis captioned "The Truth Is Out There."

"What did you say under the tree?" Tom asked. "About the future?"

"The future? The future is insects."

"Oh."

"What did you think?"

"I thought you said sex."

"Oh, I have pictures like that. I didn't want to just whip them out. Should I?"

"Sure," said Tom.

Sebastian pulled out another folder. "Look – these azure snout weevils are really going at it. Look at their feet, aren't they cute? So Dr. Seuss. And the eyestalks on her, see how they're cocked forward, you know she's thinking oh yeah baby."

Tom had to laugh.

"Wanna see more? Insects making out like mad?"

Tom watched Sebastian's face as he talked, listening not to the impenetrable flow of words as dense as a dictionary, but to the sound of excitement. These elaborate creatures lived in a complex chemical environment, Sebastian explained, where love and war are dictated by smell.

In the biochemical universe, formula is the message. And programming is attributed to an elusive, pernicious instinct. And as Sebastian says, everything he needed to know, he learned from insects.

He handed Tom a photo. "Look at this. One male mounting another male who is mating with a female. The one on top is called a superfluous male."

"A super-what?"

"A superfluous male. As far as I'm concerned," Sebastian stated, "there's no such thing."

Tom smiled. "Why not just say, threesome?"

"Yes," Sebastian said. "A tiny, marvelous threesome."

I've been there, Tom thought.

"Now where are those dragonflies?" Sebastian rummaged while he talked. "They mate in a wheel. Of course, the dragonfly is somewhat of a sexual overachiever. Males have two sexual sites. Sperm produced in one location is moved to another. And the dragonfly penis has a little scoop on the end so he can scrape out any other dragonfly sperm which happens to be there before depositing his own. Isn't that special? And she produces zillions of eggs which develop into nymphs and then morph into adults with four sets of wings. Four sets of independently functioning wings. That's how they can hover and fly backwards. Can you imagine the programming, the variable control?"

"Hang on," Tom said. "Let's get back to the dirty bits."

"They can fuck in the air."

"Oh."

"They do the wheel. He has this clamp thing on the end of his body, and her head has the groove —"

"You're making this up."

"No, really." Sebastian reached out to touch Tom's head. "Docking is high risk."

"What?"

"It's how they find each other. The clamp and groove configuration is species specific."

Tom started laughing, his arms reaching for Sebastian, who joined in laughing. Tom said, "Say it again: the tongue and groove is what?"

"The clamp and groove," Sebastian said. "The configuration is species specific."

When they stopped laughing, they were cuddling on the couch. Their warmth mingled and pooled and Tom thought, *He smells nice, what is that?*, and Sebastian thought, *I'll have to ask him not to wear fragrance.*

The smell was a barrier to mating.

Out loud, Sebastian completed his thought. "It prevents different species from interbreeding."

"What does?"

Sebastian frowned. "The clamp and groove."

"Oh that." Tom wasn't really paying attention. The most he had ever read about bugs were the instructions that came with a dark green bottle of killer shampoo. Tom decided not to mention how long he thought crabs were "public" lice. Scurrying home with his little green bottle, he felt infested, and risked permanent nerve damage leaving the shampoo on twice as long as recommended, his skin crawling from the assault. A week later, he repeated the entire process to kill any babies.

He felt itchy just remembering. Tom hoped, with a strong sudden surge of passion, that Sebastian was not going to pull out any crab sex photos. No matter how exquisitely photographed in their natural habitat, Tom did not want to see any crab sex up close. His glance rested again on the praying mantis. He was starting to find it creepy.

With little encouragement from Tom, Sebastian launched into the huge controversy surrounding praying mantises because sometimes the female will grab an approaching male and chew off his head. "It's so unfair, really," Sebastian said. "The fact is, they are programmed to ambush. That's how they do things, how they hunt, how they mate. And the ambush reflex operates from nerve bundles separate from the brain. In fact, the brain is there to second-guess the ambush reflex, to cut down on mistakes. The brain is a filter, not an originator."

They slipped down a little on the couch, their heads lolling towards each other.

"Mantids are also interesting because they are the only insects that can look over their shoulders. Poor little guys. Males try to avoid the ambush reflex by approaching from behind."

"Really? Could be fun."

"She still might grab him and chew off his head."

"So much depends on mood, doesn't it?" Tom whispered.

"And you know what? A headless male can still maneuver his body into position and carry out the mating. More evidence the male brain is really not located upstairs."

Tom laughed, and slid his hand up Sebastian's thigh.

"So the head is just a decoy." Tom pressed his lips against Sebastian's cheek. "A distraction," he said, then drew back to consider Sebastian's wide-eyed expression. "How much work would it be, to chew off a head?"

Sebastian grabbed Tom's head again in his hands and brought his face towards his own. For a moment, a long delicious moment, they both disappeared.

∞

That is the night, Sebastian likes to say, that we both lost our heads.

"Even though you smelled so bad."

"I wasn't wearing anything. Just deodorant."

"That's something. You smelled like kitty litter. You smelled like a brand new bag of kitty litter."

∞

"That first night, you were so weird," Tom recalls. "I didn't know whether to laugh or just say, oh...." (a soft moan like a puzzled sigh)

"You did both," Sebastian says.

"That's right. I did both. And you – were so weird."

"And you –" Sebastian has practiced the timing of this comeback and uses it often: "And you – liked it."

Part 2

THE SAVAGE COMMONLY FANCIES

Personal Names tabooed. – Unable to discriminate clearly between words and things, the savage commonly fancies that the link between a name and the person or thing denominated by it is not a mere arbitrary and ideal association, but a real and substantial bond which unites the two in such a way that magic may be wrought on a man just as easily through his name as through his hair, his nails, or any other material part of his person.

– J.G. Frazer, *The Golden Bough: A Study in Magic and Religion*

not sure now

They are not sure now if Sebastian had Asperger's. No
one was ever diagnosed with Asperger's syndrome when
Sebastian was young. Now, of course, it's way more
popular.

Sebastian only ever talks about it, whatever it was,
in terms of the past. If he ever had Asperger's syndrome,
it is something he's grown out of, like another kind of
adolescence (mostly) left behind.

No one can be sure. Sebastian does have his little
obsessions and his surprising fixations, but he's learned
to mask so much. He's learned to lie. Is that ironic?
He's learned to act in public and that makes him seem
much more normal. He masks so well, it makes you see
how much everyone uses masks. It's all learned, all the
basics of camouflage and communication. Sebastian
just had to learn a few simple rules of eye contact, when
and how to touch, practice a range of conversational
gambits, and now you wouldn't know, if you didn't
already.

On a good day, you might not see anything to put
your finger on. But when he gets excited or startled,
that's when you think maybe Asperger's, or even
something else. When Sebastian gets overwhelmed,

that's when he forgets himself, forgets the mask, forgets his social strategies, forgets his coping mechanisms.

When Sebastian gets overstimulated, that's when his personality starts to fragment.

Mostly, he gets excited about anything to do with bugs. And wouldn't you know it? Bugs are everywhere. Bugs are everywhere you want to look for them. Everything is a bug story, once you have that attitude and start seeing how busy life is here on bug planet.

Stupid ads on television for bug spray will set him off. He gets very excited about the bug war. He cannot watch *Starship Troopers*, not even the famous shower scene, or the whipping scene, because of their sensational treatment of the war on bugs.[5]

Now Sebastian is all excited about bisexuality, and what it means. He can be just like a baby bird with its mouth open, doing that ridiculous spasm, feed me, feed me, I need answers. What does it mean, mean, mean?

The way Sebastian functions means he can't see the simple things. All the taken-for-granted things that no one even talks about: these programming codes escape Sebastian. He just can't begin to grasp what is supposed to be obvious; especially if he's excited or confused, which is how he gets. He only understands what has become complicated, convoluted, categorized,

---

[5] Okay, maybe Sebastian can endure the shower scene. But not the whipping scene: that's gross.

and cross-referenced. He will squeeze out every shred of meaning, and then let go.

The problem with picking things apart, trying to understand them, is that at the smallest levels everything is unpredictable. There is nothing left to grasp. In the world of men, in the insect world, and indeed in the quantum world, the more you break things down into pieces and look at them, the essence becomes increasingly unknowable. In the quantum world especially, all the littlest building blocks are reported to be uniformly unpredictable. At the smallest levels, it is impossible to even distinguish between animate and inanimate.

In the face of so much uncertainty, there is no way to tell how much Sebastian really understands now about Tom, and what he just no longer gets worked up about. Is Sebastian naïve or sophisticated? Somehow, he's both. If he's both, he is beyond a label, and no question has an easy answer.

The goal, as Sebastian perceives it, is to accommodate paradox without getting overwhelmed by the onslaught of permutations and implications. The purpose of the goal is to avoid meltdowns. Sebastian remains unsure, however, how that is to be done consistently.

hard on the ego

It's all very hard on the ego, Tom muses, being the authority on so much. Being the official spokesperson for men, for bisexuals, for Buddhists, for spiritual development, for dyslexia, and for any cross-categorization of the above.

Such as "dyslexic bisexual Buddhist."

A label Tom does not like. Tom is an ego wrapped up in a body, and feeling his emotions, feeling feeling so much all the time. That is Tom.

His feelings. Your feelings. The boundaries and gradations between feelings. The source of feelings. Feeling closure. Feeling openings. Feeling his way. Tom is all about feelings.

And feeling so much sometimes when he meets someone that he absolutely must hook up with him. Sometimes Tom meets someone, usually a guy, and feels that they absolutely have to hook up. He flies into mission mode, green mission flags flying, and these high-flying green missions are hard not to notice.

Even Sebastian was only so oblivious.

∽

Justin was one of these missions. Tom had met Justin at the centre. Justin had been to India. Justin used words like "fundoo," to mean fundamentalist (said "us fundoos" meaning "U.S. fundamentalists"). Justin wore purple, was fond of everyday Sanskrit (karma, and swastika), and made a point of saying "He-MAL-ee-ya," instead of "HIM-ah-LAY-as," to signify that he had actually been there, and knew the local pronunciation. He-MAL-ee-ya. Tom found this wildly amusing, and not pretentious at all.

One of Tom's skills was enthusiasm.

Tom had not been subtle about his creeping infatuation. So casually and so persistently referenced, the significance of Justin could not have been any more blatantly ambiguous.

Ambiguity is an opening for Sebastian. He doesn't feel openings, but he uses confusion to recognize their presence.

Sparked by his brush with ambiguity, Sebastian becomes deeply fascinated with every aspect of what it means to be bisexual. What it really means. Suddenly Sebastian wants to talk about sex. The details of sex. Wants to talk about women. What is it like with a woman. What "hot and wet" meant. Inside. Really. What is that like? Hot and wet? What is juicy, Sebastian asked. In the land of lube, who knows juicy? Do you like juicy? You like it hot and juicy.

Is "juicy" a dirty word? Sebastian suddenly wanted to know. Why can't juice itself be juicy. Fruit is juicy. But juice is not. Juice is fruity, and fruit is juicy.

Squeezing and taunting, they made out like teenagers, talking dirty, brought to the brink and not touching not touching, talking of babes who are so into it, so into wanting it, they want it, want you to, hook up!

What? Tom pushed himself away.

Sebastian started laughing. And Tom wonders about the mask, and how much it has grown, and how much he is even capable of seeing. But Sebastian was laughing, so Tom laughed too.

Then they get right back to what they were doing, exploring the brink, building up to the moment, dancing along the edge of release without spilling over.

Until of course they do. Tom moaning his jagged warning, jetting wild spurts, and then Sebastian racing to catch up, Tom streaked with opalescent garnish, his eyes simmering darkly.

These are the moments which bind them to each other. There are other moments too, always more of these not-sure-now moments, these hard-on-the-ego moments, but everything quickly becomes so much less interesting and will not be revisited.

the strategy of chameleons

It was best, Sebastian had found, not to flaunt support material with a title like: *How to Make Friends*.

Sebastian had a booklet by that simple evocative name which he carried with him for years, to consult when necessary, perhaps on the bus, in order to review social strategies. Identifying an opportune moment to apply a social technique was as important as the technique itself. Application and execution were different from knowing when. When to apply and execute.

The strategy was all in the timing.

Tom was snooping a bit, and found this worn booklet in Sebastian's underwear drawer. *How to Make Friends*. Tucked away and hidden, like porn (which is what Tom was looking for).

In a way, this discovery was more shocking, and too revealing. Underneath the illustrated instructions, "How to Hug" ("Raise both arms, right arm higher than left. Place arms around partner's torso. Squeeze once gently and release"), Sebastian had written, "For a good friend, count to 5 then release."

Tom felt oddly insulted. It seemed so strategic. So calculated. He felt duped, somehow. Totally manipulated. What's worse is that all this had worked. A basic technique such as "Ask about his interests" worked on Tom, and he recognized using others ("Nod to show you are listening").

Tom had felt flattered when Sebastian asked about his yoga class or showed interest in a weekend meditation retreat. Tom always had lots to say on matters close to his heart, and Sebastian came along and pushed his buttons. Right on cue, Tom would pipe up and deliver. Feeling grateful in a way to Sebastian for the opportunity.

Was seduction really just a social formula? Was friendship entirely a matter of programming and subroutines? This means we are all faceless cogs in the gears of society.

Tom, the great chameleon seducer of both sexes, found Sebastian's brochure to be offensively strategic.

And shockingly familiar. Altogether too close to home.

When Tom has an affair with a woman, he does not mention being bisexual. Information like that is best kept on a strictly need-to-know basis. The word itself signifies a lack of commitment, a tendency to waffle (perhaps) in serious matters.

It's best not to advertise that.

With guys, Tom is bisexual. That is when he reaches for the label. In some ways, Tom thinks it adds to his cachet. Guys don't usually mind a lack of commitment, if anything they prefer it (and above all, prefer the whole topic remain unspoken). When two bisexual men engage in courtship, the challenge is to appear not that interested.

In the world of men, unavailable is the big turn-on.

Men want what they don't have. And men especially want what they can't get. That is the program to create need. And it works really well.

Tom used to say he was straight. He would flirt and cock tease and even make out, and insist he was straight. Guys are crazy for that stuff. Gay guys, are they crazy or hopeless, or what? They will do anything to make out with straight men. The experience is somehow thrilling. Maybe because the flirting is exquisitely tortuous. But how many guys can you have sex with and still call yourself straight? Is there an absolute limit?

In practice, this limit is very flexible.

For Tom, given that he was going with girls too, all the sex he was having with guys never really added up to much, even though technically the number of boys was larger than the number of girls.

The number of guys Tom had had sex with and still called himself straight was no more than ten. Not counting other straight guys, or anything ambiguous, such as that soccer player, which wasn't really making out, contact was mostly accidental, and they didn't get each other off, just got off, together. The soccer player was European, and called soccer football. It was not at all clear if he was gay. If there can be serious debate about whether oral sex is sex, then definitely two guys masturbating together, mostly not touching, some necking, is nowhere near sex. Especially if one is European, because there can be important cultural differences.

However, after no more than ten encounters with other male persons in an ad hoc frisson of frottage, hand-jobs, blow-jobs, and necking (continuing to overlook, of course, guys he has almost entirely forgotten about), and finding himself hard-boned thinking about particular assets in the world of men, Tom decided that perhaps he was after all bisexual. Of course he still liked women. He loved women. Women were everything to him. He couldn't give women up. That would be impossible, because women are an unstoppable force of nature. Women have extreme gravity. He couldn't give them up. But they could be a lot of work, and the pay-off even more work. Guys were so much easier. The sex was easier.

Sometimes Tom wondered if maybe he was bisexual because he was a little bit lazy. He didn't have to do so much work to get laid. As a straight guy having sex with men, no one expected much from him except his beauty, and perhaps his unattainability. It was easy and fun, and as zipless as a zipper, if he wanted it to be. He got off and didn't feel like he had taken advantage of anyone. He didn't take anything that wasn't freely given.

There was less guilt. Women wanted more in return; the flesh was not enough, sex was never really sex, and Tom felt guilty if he wasn't able to meet their needs. Even when their needs seemed endless. Especially if their needs seemed endless. Tom would be driven away by his own overwhelming feelings of guilt, because he could never do enough.

It took Tom years to clue in to how much he projected his own feelings onto others.

That is: a chameleon unsure of his background.

That Tom could be a dyslexic bisexual while at the same time insisting that he not be called a dyslexic bisexual was, in Sebastian's opinion, part of Tom's dyslexia. And because he was dyslexic, Tom couldn't see it this way. Could not see that what he was, was what he did not want to see.

Or maybe Tom didn't see things the same way because he was bisexual, not because he was dyslexic.

Sebastian was not sure he understood bisexual. He thought he could understand dyslexic. He could imagine dyslexic. But bisexual? To Sebastian, this seemed to be an elaborate avoidance strategy. Reaching for one thing to avoid being labeled something else.

Something worse than bisexual.

Tom never describes himself as a dyslexic bisexual, because people have snickered. He has asked Sebastian not to introduce him as a dyslexic bisexual, nor to refer to him as a dyslexic bisexual.

"Dyslexic bisexual is not my identity," Tom emphasized. "Dyslexic bisexual is not who I am."

This little speech more or less cemented things into position in Sebastian's head. Denial is the clear glue that holds everything together in plain sight. Based on what he has learned, Sebastian considered Tom to be the most outstanding dyslexic bisexual yet encountered in the wild.

The world of men is not about men. It is about being a man. In the world of men, a strange unpredictable place, being a man is all about the individual. In the world of men, each individual was, paradoxically, representative and unique. Each individual could be so different, and yet, perhaps, typical.

There was no real way to tell who was what.

Before becoming world famous for his research into human sexual behaviour, Alfred C. Kinsey was first of all an entomologist, and his specialty was gall wasps. He collected thousands of galls, shipping them back to his laboratory to wait for the wasps to emerge (the wasps were then killed for science). Each gall, a deformed section of plant, swollen like a bulb, was a nest of wasp pupae. To study insects properly, large populations must be sampled. Entomology was all about large numbers. Insects and statistics are made for each other.

As a relentless and professional zoologist, Kinsey then applied the same rigorous sampling techniques to the study of human sexuality, and eventually compiled thousands of histories and developed what became known as the Kinsey scale. The Kinsey scale was science and sex combined. A scale or a continuum serves to blur distinctions, and the seven-point Kinsey scale gathers us all together in one place, spread out somewhere between a zero (heterosexual) and a six (homosexual).

There was no way Sebastian could survey enough individuals to determine how men were the same and in what ways different. In the world of men, Sebastian faced severely restricted research parameters, and doubted he would ever be able to gather meaningful data.

Sebastian's extremely limited research sample was Tom. Tom says he is a perfect Kinsey three, neither homo nor hetero, and yet somehow both.

Findings may not be representative, but Sebastian has reached certain conclusions based on the evidence to date. Tom was a dyslexic bisexual. One of the finest specimens an independent researcher could ever hope to encounter. Yet one who expressed displeasure with the phrase which closely identified him. Tom had firmly requested that the words "dyslexic bisexual" not even be so much as whispered in his presence.

"Or," he said, "ever."

"Ever?" Sebastian felt discouraged at the enormity of this request.

"Yes. Please." Tom was obviously trying very hard suddenly to be nice. "Please never say those words. Like that."

"Like what?"

"You know. Together."

"Okay," said Sebastian. In his head, the reddish-blue words echoed: *Dys-lexic Bi-sexual. Dys-lexic Bi-sexual.*

Tom's brown eyes swimming.

"Okay," Sebastian said again. "Okay." But the words had stuck together in Sebastian's head, bound in an undeniably clear glue, and the best he could do to honour Tom's request was to never say the words out loud, so that Tom could hear.

a backwards glance

Sebastian can remember the day he realized he had
a body and was inside it. He realized he was alone
inside his body and always would be. And not only was
Sebastian alone inside his body: everyone was alone
inside. Everyone was separate and alone inside and
none of these people knew any better than Sebastian.
None of them had much of a clue what was happening
inside anyone else. All of us are alone inside our
fragments of existence, and would be until we die, and
who knows what happens then.[6]

When Sebastian realized how we were, each of us,
separate, the body that he was alone inside was about
fifteen years old and male. No one else could ever
know what it was like to be inside there, alone with
the echoes of Sebastian's universe, alone at the shaky
centre of awkward limbs dusted red-gold. Sebastian
realized he was alone inside a fifteen-year-old gold-

---

[6] Maybe at death each of us is still alone, but in another, different
way. The whole secret, according to Tom, is knowing when you
are dead, and to be prepared for this transition at each and every
moment. Apparently if you die, but fail to recognize that you are
dead, this is a big problem.

touched youth. He had not totally realized this before, had not seen so much to be true in this way. He was becoming something else. He was becoming who he would be despite himself.

This was the day that Sebastian realized he could never look at himself. Except through a mirror, he could never see his own face. Only in the mirror was he outside. Outside gave perspective. In the mirror he saw someone he might be. He was blond. He had cheekbones. His eyebrows were darker at their base.

He reached out and touched the cool hand meeting his.

In the mirror, he puzzled over who was in there, under the gold-tipped fur strewn across his brow. The mirror helped him to see, although, as Tom tends to do, Sebastian may have gotten everything backwards.

Tom's theories about love

A quick, fortuitous, and fortifying affair is like a vaccination against the madness. People fall in love through sheer physical pleasure. They become skin drunk, as Tom calls it.

And a one-night stand, or several of them, or a couple of short, intense *physical* affairs was like a flu shot against the slippery slope of that madness, although just like the flu shot it only protected against familiar things. This approach only protects against certain known variants, projected from previous exposures.

Tom had had a lot of experience in the world of men, but experience did not prepare him for Sebastian. There always remains in the world the shock of the completely unprecedented.

Despite repeated vaccinations against the madness of the flesh, and some fear that he was addicted to the cure, Tom still became mildly afflicted with bouts of delirium and other symptoms of the skin drunk madness.

Tom may appear world-weary and detached, but at the same time he is interested in his world, and not detached at all but very attached. He is completely attached.

Attached to distractions. And to the entire process of letting go of distractions. And then interested in other distractions, to distract him from those distractions which he has just let go of completely.

After meeting Sebastian, Tom suddenly became very fond of this girl he'd known for some time but never really pursued, and also thoroughly nailed some hippie boy with mousy dreads he'd met at the coffee shop. The kid came back for more and still Tom felt the symptoms of madness, a craving for something else, something back and forward in time, something sideways (next to him) called Sebastian.

Tom could not stop thinking about the texture of Sebastian's short, straight hair, even while he nailed that dreaded hippie boy for a second time. In fact, it was right then and there, buried in some brand spanking new matted-hair large-boned wrinkle-browed puppy moaning his fool head off, in that moment of Tom's life, he realized his mind was full of dragonflies, and that was a sign from the universe.

It had to be.

The dragonflies had to be a sign of something.

The sign was hazy, but Tom was utterly convinced

that maybe something, something, would become of those dragonflies in his head. Something had possessed him, and he needed to dive right into the middle of that to see what it was.

It was not skin drunkenness this time. He was confronted with some sort of other situation.

And so Tom continued to do what he has always done: vigorously pursued the pleasures of the "fresh." He threw himself into a frenzy of fucking the hippie boy, and yet still thought of dragonflies, mating in a wheel.

"Males have two sexual sites," Tom murmured, and then froze, realizing that he had spoken out loud.

The kid moaned. "Huh?"

Tom throbbed his cock muscle. "Sweet ass, dude."

The kid bit down on a mouthful of matted braids.

Sperm produced in one location is moved to another, Tom thought, as he filled the reservoir tip of a large waterslide-lubed condom planted in the hippie boy. The warmth of the boy's muscular core surrounded him.

Bugs are strange. Tom's weight melted down into the large-boned young man beneath him, and his thoughts flowed away, and beyond.

Mating in a wheel.

straight to high school

Tom was informed that he had a learning disability.

Otherwise, if someone hadn't come right out and told him, he might never have caught on.

Tests had disclosed that Tom had a sequencing disorder and marked transpositional tendencies.

In another word, he was dyslexic.

He got things backwards.

In a way, Tom knew this already. Although it had never been pointed out, he had discovered this in his own way. Often in math he would have the right numbers, but not in the right order. To Tom, this was "almost right." Having the right numbers was almost right; having these numbers in a particular order did not seem as important. Nothing to get bent out of shape about.

Almost right was pretty good. It was close to perfect.

Now, almost right meant he was dyslexic.

And this was supposedly related to Tom being left-handed.

When the home schooling option had been utterly exhausted and Tom went straight to high school, all these issues arose at more or less the same time.

∽

Being left-handed was nothing until Tom went to school. He never even realized that such a thing as favouring one hand over the other for a particular task, such as writing, was so significant that it required a name. When he picked up a pen or pencil, he used his left hand. When he weeded the turnips, he used both hands as necessary. When he jerked off, he was equally versatile.

Tom learned so much about names and stigma when he went to school.

He learned he was left-handed, and that there was an attitude left over apparently from the Dark Ages that left-handedness was wrong and ought to be discouraged.

One teacher phoned his parents, or tried to, but in the process talked to several Farm animals, each of whom claimed involvement as family and took the opportunity to express their feelings about Om-Taraka[7] being blessed with two hands and who on earth was to say right and wrong between them. Om-Taraka can be whatever he wants to be, Mrs. Cahill was told. He was never called left-handed on the Farm; we saw the tendency, but saw no reason to even name it, much less

_____

[7] Tom's original birth name, later changed.

judge it as improper. One hand is as good as the other, if the heart is pure.

Tom remembers Mrs. Cahill encouraging him to try, just try, to write with his right hand. The *right* one, she'd gently emphasize, and he would try. He would really try. But Tom couldn't write with his right hand any more than he could eat with his right hand. He felt retarded whenever he tried to use his right hand. He would starve for sure if he had to rely on his right hand to move food towards his face.

He painstakingly wrote with his right hand to placate Mrs. Cahill, but he wasn't good at it. It didn't feel natural, and the result was not pleasing.

Mrs. Cahill's anticipated breakthrough never arrived. Unamused by his slow, illegible performance, she stopped her efforts at correcting Tom, although she remained disturbed at the sight of him, twisted askew in the right-handed desk, his scribbler balanced on his knee, writing (it seemed to her) upside down.

Obviously the sequencing disorder, the tendency to transpose letters and numbers, the left-handed upside-down backwardness: all of these were somehow related.

Mrs. Cahill wondered what else might be wrong.

That was so clearly the problem with home schooling. By the time the kids came through the doors of high school, there was nothing more to be done with them.

Tom went straight to high school.

High school is where Tom discovered girls, in a way he never had before.

There was a fresh crop of boys at high school too, but Tom didn't discover boys then, not in the same way he discovered girls. Tom had already been swimming in a liquid sea of boys, and as much as Tom discovered girls, and kept discovering girls, boys were always with him. He was never left or right-handed with another boy, because who cared? Bisexual boys are naturally ambidextrous.

Tom never left the boys behind. They were with him as he bedded each woman, and they were ahead of him waiting, hungry and nurturing, if he ever stumbled or needed a pick-me-up.

Or a complete change of pace.

Whatever. The boys were always there for Tom.

Girls he discovered in high school, at the same time he discovered he was left-handed.

And dyslexic.

And bisexual too, if you want to start throwing out all the labels. Even ones Tom did not use yet.

Tom also discovered, in high school, that he was from an outlandish place called the Farm, which was not quite as simple and straightforward as the name mplied.

In high school, Tom learned that the Farm was really some kind of weird hippie commune. He definitely qualified as an outcast, being one of them Jesus freaks and all, except he was so easy-going and cute that everything not overlooked was forgiven.[8] His origins were not held against him, but the swelling breasts of town girls were. In addition, bending to the prevailing attitude about what the hippie freaks were up to out at their "farm," Tom became a small-time drug dealer. The product line reflected agricultural roots and user-friendly prices. Local and organic, grass, magic mushrooms. The fruits of Mother Earth available in season.

This carefree entrepreneurial spirit ended up being why Tom was expelled from the weird hippie commune.

He had overlooked the importance of sharing, although there were definitely other issues as well. The traffic in hallucinogens was one thing, but more serious was the breach of the community goal of openness. "That was the nail they hung it on," Tom said. "That I had been deceitful about what I was doing."

An unspoken issue was the surplus of young males in the commune. Older males were establishing harems of wives, and young unattached men were a threat to the institutional stability of polygamy. Worked like slaves while young and strong, at the first sign of rebellion or frustration, or if there was any sort of attitude problem, such as imagining having a woman of one's own to

---

[8] Tom claims that their reputation as "Jesus freaks" came about because the Farm, as camouflage, made a point of quoting the words of Jesus during encounters with townspeople and outsiders. The Farm felt they were better off branded as "Jesus freaks" rather than more accurately labelled as pantheistic, and embracing paganism, animism, and permissiveness.

pursue a pair bond, such freethinking young men would be invited to leave the Farm.

Tom was invited to leave.

Freedom, Tom says, is just another word for doing things my way.

what does Tom

Tom thinks that every man is a little bit gay. That is what makes the concept so dangerous. That is why it must be suppressed.

What does Tom think about?
    The boy who got away.
    The next boy.
    The boy next door.
    The boys down the hall.
    Couples. Even though Tom says he is over couples, he still thinks about couples. Straight couples. A male/female couple. Sometimes a couple is sexier than either of its elements. That is why couples interested Tom in the first place. The synergy. But what works for two may not accommodate a perfect three. The triangle is a different power configuration. There is also the guy factor. Straight guys love looking at other men, and men who are into it love watching another man fuck the wife, so to speak. It makes her hotter. Some men are so into this, heating up the wife by having a cute guy

fuck her; and yet they will maintain clear boundaries, will not in any way touch the man who fucks the wife. Is that not most peculiar? With a couple like this, the woman is in between the two guys, and that is not what Tom wanted. He wanted to be as close to the guy. But the girlfriend was too often in between the men, and sometimes in the way.

The trouble with couples, eventually, is that they will discover that they are really, actually, more into each other than into you. Plus there's that guy thing, and how much the guy is even into other guys. They could be really great people, but it was just a game for the couple, and Tom no more than a toy.

Couples became a game that Tom knew he could never win. He could play all he wanted, and score all over the place, but never win.

Tom felt gayer with a couple sometimes than he ever did when totally naked and vulnerable and open to another man. With a couple, there is always the third person to witness who sucks cock. Compared to a super-straight guy, Tom was as gay as a penguin (and needed to conceal this), even though, perversely, the super-straight guy found it hot watching Tom fuck his wife (a good activity to camouflage gayness). There was something about Tom's lean cuteness that straight guys wanted, but did not dare touch. They reached for him through their women, but did not reach far enough for Tom.

Does any of this make sense?

Do you know who Tom is now?

He gave up couples because they turned out to be twice the work, but he still thinks about them. Straight couples with synergy remain attractive.

Tom was straight for a while in his early twenties. He had outgrown sex with boys, just like he had outgrown his banana seat bike, his mohair goats, and the fierce communion with owls which consumed him when he was ten.

He grew up, and as far as he knew he was straight. Tom was as normal as the spawn of hippie freaks ever could be. He had girlfriends. He wanted to get married. The world was a beautiful place.

Couples were Tom's way of reaching out again to other men sexually. The approach was oblique, and dating straight couples did not in the end take Tom as far as he wanted to go. He then started fuck-buddy dating a number of available men; that was another phase, and fun, but he soon tired of it. Tom also slowly became aware of feeling a kind of nurturing instinct, or compulsion, which made him want to reach out to young men and take them into his arms. He wanted them to rest there, like a memento.

In summary then, Tom dropped straight guys, started fuck-buddy dating his peers, and reached out to younger men who needed a minute's nurturing.

And of course, through all of this Tom had a

girlfriend. Not always the same one, but always one with severe gravity.[9]

It must be noted that much of what Tom talks about is, as he says, "all behind me now." What does Tom expect to be talking about five years from now?

---

[9] Severe gravity might be the same as extreme gravity. Tom also talks about women having "biological" gravity. Here, gravity does not mean seriousness, but refers to a mysterious force in the universe.

symptoms of confusion

It is difficult to be sure what exactly is a symptom of confusion.

So much of what Sebastian was totally confused about (such as the meaning of life, or why a man would shave his armpits) turns out to be uncertain anyway. Everyone is confused about these things. So Sebastian has every reason to be confused. It was only natural, after all. Being confused was the human condition: why was Sebastian being singled out?

Confusion was as natural as breathing.

So in that context, what is a symptom of confusion? Sebastian remains unsure. Is a symptom of confusion the same as confusion itself?

Confusion itself eludes capture.

Confusion is never a straightforward destination. Confusion can be a mask for something else, for ignorance, or fear, or denial. So then the challenge becomes, how to recognize confusion? Is this fear masking as confusion, or confusion as the face of denial?

Since symptoms of confusion have become a symptom of Sebastian's condition, confusion has become a state of mind Sebastian is often not willing to recognize.

Thoreau said all men live lives of quiet desperation.[10]

And Sebastian wondered if that just about summed it up.

Perhaps that is what it is like for many people. A quiet desperation, which they quietly endure.

And Sebastian wondered why he was the one with the possible diagnosis and the likely syndrome, since he felt perfectly fine (most of the time) just the way he was. It was all these other people, all those normal, well-adjusted people who were beyond diagnosis: all those normal people normally felt miserable.

Or at least that was the way they acted. Not confused at all. Definitely miserable.

And Sebastian wasn't confused either. Not really. Not about little things. Only about big things. Big unanswerable things.

---

[10] Sebastian is grateful he never had to "learn" English. Otherwise, he would not be able to get through a phrase such as "live lives" with his composure intact.

What Sebastian felt therefore was normal confusion.

Whenever Sebastian contemplated the human condition, he tended to relate events to something comparable in the insect world.

Who lives and who dies; who is encouraged and who is squashed: all of these things are mysterious to Sebastian.

When Sebastian hears of the Inquisition, or ongoing religious intolerance, he thinks of insect atrocities. He is not surprised by what people do to each other considering what they do to insects. Thousands of precious little field spiders have been roasted alive, so that their ashes could be rubbed on those hoping to be as lithe and nimble. Does no one ever point a finger at the pagans?

Who laments today the passing of the passenger pigeon louse, untold millions of which perished with the extinction of their hosts.

Insect atrocities: the untold story. Don't get Sebastian going.

altar project

Tom speaks of his altars. All Sebastian has to do is keep
still long enough and Tom will tell him all about altars.
His favorite altars, altars he sometimes misses, altars
he's been thinking of for some time.

Altars are living and therefore evolve. The altar is
something to maintain and also something to be talked
about. Through this attention, the altar becomes a
vehicle of self-exploration and display.

The story of Tom's life can be told through the
altars he has maintained. Tom reminisces about
particular altars. The snake altar in the southwest
corner. Padma Sambhava, who follows him everywhere
but always keeps changing. The owl altar when Tom
was ten, decorated with the feathers he found once he
started saving them. Saving them for the altar. They
were not all from owls, of course, and he didn't even
pretend they were, but the feathers all found a home
on the owl altar. Black on one side, and mostly white
on the other, and the brownish-grey stripy ones in the
middle like a bouquet. Three precious blue ones in
front. For a while, when his faith in the owl altar had
been at its peak, Tom found feathers everywhere. And
heard owls in the night. He always knew they were

there, and the altar their real home.

Tom tells different stories laying down. More spills out of Tom when he is horizontal and the lights are dim. What spills out is not linear, but is oddly captivating: *snake worship season* is seriously discussed at length. Tom snuggles closer into Sebastian and says snake worship season is really about snake worshippers. Tom's whispers in the dark explode inside Sebastian's head like the gentlest of purple bombs. Words that Tom whispers in the dark are almost always purple or blue or teal, and flicker softly as they expand outwards and fade into the silence of listening to each other breathe. A cocoon of white noise, punctuated by a faint whistling out of Tom's nose streaking an ochre echo across Sebastian's landscape.

Sebastian wonders how much he will ever really know about Tom. No matter how much he really tried to listen. So much flows past and remains mysterious. Curled up in a spoon, or falling asleep draped over Tom's back, wondering what was going on inside this large warm beautiful affectionate animal.

Sebastian, it seems, is always wondering how much anyone can ever know what it is like to be another. Since he has started sleeping with Tom, this distance Sebastian feels between him and the rest of the animal population has become, simultaneously, as thin as a mingled layer of sweat, and as gaping as the inconceivable muddle we struggle to navigate.

In the midst of this, Sebastian remains alert to symptoms of confusion.

Altars are a means of recognizing that there is something one wishes to recognize as being worthy in the first place of having an altar in recognition of it. This is not exactly what Tom said about altars, but a fairly accurate synopsis.

An altar, Tom says, represents the intersection between the focus of the idea symbolized by the actual altar, and the influence of that idea as it moves through your life. An altar has the double gravity of a physical location and a spiritual address. Every thought, every idea, must pass the scrutiny of an ideally located altar.

Tom's words shower bursts of teal across Sebastian's horizon. This is the greenhouse effect. Whenever Tom is around. From all the hot air.

Part 3

THE BEGINNINGS OF SEX

The soldiers' odor of sweat – that odor like
a sea breeze, like the air, burned to gold,
above the seashore – struck my nostrils
and intoxicated me. This was probably
my earliest memory of odors. Needless
to say, the odor could not, at that time,
have had any direct relationship with
sexual sensations, but it did gradually and
tenaciously arouse within me a sensuous
craving for such things as the destiny of
soldiers, the tragic nature of their calling,
the distant countries they would see, the
ways they would die....

– Yukio Mishima, *Confessions of a Mask*

two people is magic

Two people is magic, is something Tom would say.
Two people is magic, is something Tom has said, many times.

But what he means by that, he won't say.
Oh sure, he tries to explain. He will talk a long time by way of an explanation, but won't say that much.
It is, apparently, supposed to be obvious. Two people is magic. Magic is two people.
Tom seems comfortable with the word. Although present (and earnestly alert) on occasions described as magic, it is never quite clear to Sebastian what this diagnosis entails. What *exactly*.
Two people is magic, according to Tom.
The truth of this statement is self-evident, according to Tom. Two people is magic; magic is two people.
At least two people.

the smell of love

Tom has a great smell. Tom smells really really good. When Tom is fresh out of the bath, scrubbed down with unscented products, Sebastian just wants to bury his face into Tom and smell the smell.

Sebastian wants to wrap himself all around Tom and bury himself in the smell. Tom's smell. There is no other way to describe the smell, except to say, he loves the smell of Tom.

The smell of love may not be smells you love.

Tom smells like the planet.

Tom smells like the earth and dirt and ocean and the sun.

Tom smells like gas.

Tom smells of salt and seaweed and sometimes he smells bitter. A sharp bitterness wafting from soft ponds. The planet Tom smells like has sewers and dumps, as well as waterfalls and hidden gardens.

Sebastian likes armpits, still to this day, but has learned not to mention them as much as he thinks about them. An armpit is all-terrain, mountains and valleys and foothills, and looks best if not clear-cut.

⚭

Putting aside the smell issue, and Sebastian knows just how hard that can be, Sebastian does not understand why more people do not love the armpit. He does not understand why "armpit of the world" is not a recommendation. Even if people are not total bagpipers, it should be naturally easy to love the armpit because it is beautiful. People love the chest. People love arms. The armpit is both chest and arm. Plus the hair and shadow-mystery of crotch. The ribs underneath smiling.

The armpit was everything all at once.

⚭

It is clear that what Sebastian likes most is looking at armpits. Is that queer? Looking at armpits?

Looking at armpits was best because the smell could be too much. In a way, it was like a face. A face can be too much to look at. There is too much going on. The smell of an armpit could also be too much. But the sight of a good armpit was perfect. The sight of an armpit conveys the sensation of intoxication without actual impairment.

Sebastian quite liked looking at armpits. Armpits are as expressive and individual as any face. They are more beautiful and less confusing. And, as a bonus, armpits have the double sexiness of twins. Armpits are like a pair of hidden bonsai gardens. For Sebastian, the armpit was the key to unlocking the appreciation of beauty.

Armpits make perfect visuals, for the very same reason that autopsies are best on television: the smell.[11]

Tom's smell for some reason has not become too much. Mostly it is quite nice, although not always. Something about Tom's smell, which Sebastian cannot identify, has provoked the following questions:

"How many levels of communication, conscious and unconscious, are going on simultaneously?"

"Is smell the catch in this lock?" Sebastian asks, his arms wrapped around Tom. Chesting from behind. The metaphor may seem scrambled, because it has been translated into consciousness, from wherever these things exist before they are words.

Before being translated into words.

"Does smell trigger love?" The entomologist needs to know. "Does smell make love happen?"

---

[11] Forensic entomology as a career path for Sebastian, although initially appealing, was not possible due to the prevalence of strong, overwhelming odours.

The dirtiest words in Sebastian's juvenile world when an armpit, a manly boy bush, became everything: "arm crotch." Arm crotch was whispered when Sebastian first tried talking dirty (with himself). Arm crotch became the point of entry which led Sebastian into the world of men.

"Arm crotch" is still a good thing to say. It makes Tom laugh.

"You want to do *what* with my arm crotch?" Tom had asked.

Until he met Sebastian, Tom had never even heard of bagpiping, and is generally too ticklish to be really good at it. He is generous displaying the twins. He calls one, "Hidden bonsai garden number one," and the other, "Also, hidden bonsai garden number one."

This kind of nonsense really amuses Tom.

the beginnings of sex

Tom cannot recall when he started having sex. Tom was somehow never pre-sexual. He can remember early experiences, but not the beginnings of sex.

Sebastian started having sex in high school.

Sebastian's initiation into sex became dramatic only in retrospect. His sex life started with a blow-job, but Sebastian did not realize in high school that it was not that typical to receive your first blow-job from your math teacher. It was like growing up in the Age of Innocence and not even knowing it, and hence the declarative capitals.

The math teacher, Mr. Davies, was popular and seemed incredibly old, even though he was in his twenties. He was disheveled. He listened. He laughed. He chatted.

Some guys dropped by where he lived.

They began to call him Bill. They began to say things like, yeah Bill, go for it.

Bill smiled and laughed while he told these stories.

This was not a one-shot deal. Sebastian came back
for more. Mr. Davies also provided access to a web of
gossip and intrigue that Sebastian had not imagined
existed. Many stories were impossible to believe at first,
but then, who could ever have predicted that Mr. Davies
would give him a rum and coke, suck him off but good,
and then feel like chatting about other boys who were
into this sort of thing. It was astonishing. Boys were
"going" with each other, even some of the popular boys
at his very own high school.

Sebastian was totally out of the loop.

Except for what he was learning from the blow-job
teacher.

Sebastian gazed at these popular popular boys with
fresh eyes, stunned by the possibilities. A whole new
dimension of being had been revealed.

Sebastian was especially fascinated by the captain
of the basketball team, a tall blond confident jock with
a friendly smile who was supposed to be screwing
everything with a pulse.

Everything but Sebastian, beating and beating,
the air around him quivering, cut by intense rainbow
streaks, the ricocheting shouts of boys echoing in a riot,
vibrating, shaken and suffused by the penetrating odour
of locker rooms, armpits, and team captains.

The captain of the basketball team is Sebastian's first bisexual crush, that is, his first crush on a known bisexual, that is, someone who was sexual with males and females, although of course, such a person is often actually straight all along.

turn-ons

It is a fact that Sebastian, especially when thinking or staring, appears slightly cross-eyed.

It is also true that Sebastian spends much of his time thinking and staring.

Although wildly inaccurate, school kids called Sebastian "Bug-Eyes."

Teased and taunted, Sebastian stopped looking directly at people. It was easier that way anyway. People made him uncomfortable: their faces kept changing and he could not keep up. Eyes were too much. Lips were too much. At best he could manage a quiet detail, like the row of stubble left on a cheek as the high water mark of shaving. Sebastian could see a detail like that, *or* talk, but not both.

It was easier to use a gentle gaze, looking out the sides of unfocussed eyes. Four eyes is what he had, two in front and two to the sides. They all worked if he felt like it. If he felt like seeing. If he could relax and hold the vision.

Most of the time he didn't. Faces trapped him, and

then he couldn't function. He couldn't see a face and talk at the same time.

Tom's reaction to Sebastian was, of course, different. If not too expositive to mention: you can always count on Tom's reaction being different.

To Tom, the way Sebastian looked was a huge turn-on.

Slightly cross-eyed was hot. And Sebastian's wrists were spectacular. Sebastian's wrists and forearms seemed thicker than the rest of him, denser, packed with jutting bones and forested with golden fur rippling with underground rivers.

Tom actually said, way too early in the relationship, "I love your wrists."

It was the first time the word "love" had been spoken, and it hung there in the universe between them heavy and resonant. A purple splotch. Sebastian impressed himself by not even trying to say anything. He just stared at Tom, smiling, slightly cross-eyed, and Tom inched forward. "I mean," Tom said, "they're really beautiful. They make me want to kiss you."

"My wrists?" Sebastian asked.

"You," Tom said. "All of you."

The word "kiss" as it came off Tom's lips was a kind of blue that melted from the edges and faded, but lingered.

The word "Tom" also became bluer after this. *Thoughts* of Tom were oddly tinged blue somehow, in a new development.

And "blue" itself became infused with an aura of eroticism.

So much so that at times the sky threatens to overwhelm with the enormity, and Sebastian looks to the ground, for stability.

Tom, he thinks, swimming in blue, *is both ground and sky. And what changes is where I am. And what I am looking at, in my head.*

expository sequence

The thing about Tom and Sebastian is that they are many things. They can be different things, depending how you look at them.

Sebastian has identified that Tom is drawn to large-eyed, fine-featured pretty boys (not that there is anything wrong with that). Given any sort of opportunity, that is what Tom selects for recreational bonding.

What Tom prefers for pair bonding, from what Sebastian has been able to observe, are age-mates, male or female, who are more or less his equivalent in several significant regards. They can mirror him without being him. Different, but equal.

It astounds Sebastian that, as far as Tom is concerned, such a person could be male or female. It is very mysterious how Tom can be so flexible and accommodating in his requirements. The code word used is "versatile."

Sebastian also does not quite see how *he* fits in this category of different, but mirroring. Sebastian, obviously, was just different. Could not Tom detect this? Perhaps there was something wrong with Tom. Much seems to escape him, or else it is true that he just doesn't care. In a good way. Tom is obviously just not as obsessed about the same things to the same degree that Sebastian is. And that's okay.

Sebastian feels compelled to note that in his relations with Tom, he, Sebastian, was the top. The top in the sexual dimension, as he more or less always is, in the sexual dimension.

With the large-eyed pretty boys, Tom is the top. That is the whole point of the exercise. He is the man who knows what he wants and gets it. He seduces them; he *has* them. Once they've been had, they are less attractive. Which is okay, because the young oscillate at such high frequencies, they have already moved on.

With women, Tom's the top, or at least, the nominal top.

This one aspect of the ultimate act does not define sexuality, yet so often is used as the summing up. The top/bottom thing defines very little, but is used to say so much.

It confounded Sebastian a bit, it did, that he expressed his gayness by admiring the beauty of men and mounting them when possible, while Tom expressed his sexual nature as both top and bottom, and ends up being, somehow, less gay overall than someone who just stands up and says I'm gay, I screw boys.

Tom screws boys and girls, so ends up less gay. All that screwing makes everything less significant.

And yet, the ultimate act itself is extremely expository.

So what does all this mean, in terms of looking at Tom and Sebastian, and taking a perspective on what is happening?

Yes, that is a question.

It means simply that all this is happening, and Sebastian must find a way to write a few things down.

Tom isn't really gay, for example: that needs to be mentioned. That needs looking at. Especially since Tom repeatedly craves some individual naked male attention from an age-mate who is his equivalent in several significant regards.

It is baffling to contemplate that such numinous bonding rituals are solemnly conducted by men who consider themselves "straight-acting." Straight-acting involves much same-sex activity.

Maybe that is the secret to understanding: the definition must be broadened. Straight-acting means everything. Even things more strictly defined as "gay-doing" rather than "straight-acting." The gay-doing covers a small part, and the straight-acting covers the rest of it.

In a mysterious process more emotional than mathematical, in the bent world of straight men, one girlfriend (anywhere, anytime) can cancel out any number of boyfriends.

Sebastian finds it hard to keep a straight face in the world of men. Men are either desirable or ridiculous. Never both.

Sebastian will only examine a few things. A few threads of meaning. Due to time constraints, a focus must be maintained. Focus is everything.

He will write down as much as possible. However, this will only be a few fragmented memories. He will not even try to write everything down, for that would be impossible.

That would be like trying to learn everything in the world of insects which, if not strictly impossible, is highly, highly unlikely. It is a dream that will never come true.

sex with Tom

We necked so much at first. There was also so much talking. We just kind of laid around, sprawled on top of each other, and talked.

And necked.

And kept talking. We talked around our erections. We told stories that did not involve us having sex as part of the narrative thrust. Sebastian had no time to wonder what to do, because there was so much easy talking.

And necking.

Eventually there would have to be talk of sex. Eventually there was talk of sex, and then there was some sex, and then more sex. But it took weeks before the ultimate act in the world of men was actually performed.

So much in the world of men is actually about courtship and romance and *feeling*: the feeling of carrying this other man in your heart, and in your body. So little is actually about an ultimate act. Nonetheless, the inevitable discourse is framed around ultimate acts, one perhaps about to happen, or one which may have

already happened in mythic time and therefore reigns
super-influential, yet subtle.

Well, weeks went by and the ultimate act never
happened. Not with Tom and Sebastian.

Something else had to happen first.

Tom, you see, was sending mixed messages
concerning: his desire to be mounted by Sebastian; his
inclination to have anyone mount him; his impatience
with the whole topic (which he dwelled on); and
his marked possessiveness if Sebastian so much as
whispered "Nice jeans" about a pair sauntering past.

That is when Tom most wanted to be wanted.
When those jeans sauntered by. He wanted to catch
Sebastian's eye and be desired. He wanted to be swept
up by that look.

But first, Tom's journey had to take him past another
marker before looping back to Sebastian. Tom's journey
involved a dramatic tableau, some tricks and logistics,
and a stylized, ritualized performance as nuanced as
anything out of kabuki.

Before he could find his way to Sebastian, Tom
first had to be seen fucking another man. A boy really,
a long-haired skater boy. Tom arranged this spectacle,
and Sebastian witnessed the scene. The scene was
intended to convey the message that young men such as
this were part of Tom's life. Sebastian could plainly see
what was going on. The boy was pretty but hard-eyed
already, and did not seem to mind being displayed with

his legs in the air. Hair falling over one side of his face. Surprisingly deep moans pounded out of him. Dark, knowing, greedy moans. Sebastian closed the door when he had had enough.

So Sebastian knew what he was getting into. He knew about the boys from the beginning. He thought, *Tom can do better.* There were better boys for Tom. Private boys, who Sebastian would never so much as glimpse but already knew about in a queer way. Through Tom.

Once he had witnessed the scene, once he had been so informed of Tom's passion, establishing Tom as a nominal top, then it was okay for Sebastian to mount Tom.

Which he did. Rather a lot there for a while.

And that lasted for about six weeks.

People have asked, "Hey, how did you guys get together?"

The answer to that question is also mostly found within those same six weeks.

And what happened was sex with Tom.

Sex with Tom, and a projection of the life span of a golden parachute. Golden here like golden topping. Also a euphemism for something pretending to be what it was not. Golden topping was not butter, a golden shower was not like bathing in gold, and a golden parachute was not the promise of an easy landing.

What happened was sex with Tom, unexpectedly *sleeping* with Tom, and the critical perils of a tin parachute. In a state of calm panic, Sebastian agreed to move.

It was not the best time, but it was time. So he moved.

Into a neutral space where they each had room.

That is how they came to live together.

And after that, neither one of them ever really moved out.

Not entirely.

Not for long.

sensitive boys

Tom has many experiences with sensitive boys. He doesn't care if they are straight or gay, he just talks to them. Talks about art, or beauty, or love.

And then screws the bejesus out of them. He'll talk about art and beauty, especially their art, but never their beauty, then nail them over the back of a convertible futon bed. It was amazing, how it happened. Tom had a total sincere empathy for sensitive puppies. Tom was all about sensitive. He knew the mixture of idealism and despair which brought puppies to their knees.

Tom was all over sensitive boys, and it didn't really matter if they were gay or straight. All sensitive boys seem to crave some stiffening: of the spine, of the will, whatever. They love it. Sensitive boys crave being desired, that is the biggest thing. Sensitive boys have been too nice for too long, and without knowing how to ask for it crave a simultaneous initiation, defilement, and liberation. These manboys grew from Tom's strength like a tree grows from the root. The erection, once planted, prods and stiffens and the boy grows into himself. Just like a puppy grows into his paws.

Sensitive boys aren't always sensitive, Tom says. But they always remember being sensitive.

Tom liked the idea of an ass that had never been fucked before.

There was something about an ass that had never been fucked which called to Tom. The idea attracted him more than anything. An ass which had never been fucked before did not know how to express itself, and yet it knew enough to call to Tom.

An ass that knew what it wanted and pushed for it had less appeal. An ass like that never turned out to be attached to someone Tom ever developed much of a crush on.

Tom embraced impermanence because there was no future in any particular sensitive boy. There were just more and more sensitive boys, a never-ending parade, each one promising more.

More of whatever it was that Tom was looking for.

Each one more ephemeral.

And each one, perversely, more beautiful.

different similarities

What Sebastian sought was a kind of reliable, straightforward maleness that was outside himself. Sebastian wanted a man who reflected what Sebastian could be or could become.

What Sebastian sought was a different similar, a better half who was inspiration, template, and guide.

This is both similar to, and different from, Tom's requirement for a different equal.

What Tom sought was at least two things, and that was just with men. Tom was, in the vernacular, a top and a bottom. Tom deserved to be called bisexual for that accomplishment alone. He was versatile; his sexual terrain extended all the way from other men to relaxed, athletic, outdoorsy women.

Some of Tom's younger conquests in the world of men are emphatically androgynous, with one-syllable male-ish names like Chad or Bryce. Maybe just their youth made them androgynous. Tom's influence, he said, was to help them form, to take shape, to become. To become something other than bait for control freaks, tyrants, and predators. Opposites attract, do they not? The androgyne attracts the alpha male, each drunk on testosterone. This scene often is not as pretty as it may sound.

Tom of course is not a control freak, a tyrant, or a predator. He is a helper. A selfless teacher. A generous mentor. He rushes to get in there first with his special vaccination, preparing the boys for the future, trying to protect them from the worst; turning boys into men, or at least, turning boys face down, at first, for a back massage.

And that is what Tom emphasizes. Sometimes, he says, a back massage is just a back massage. This throws the boys off, because everyone wants to be seduced, right? Every boy is vain. Boys are the vainest creatures on earth, except for girls, and if you don't make a pass, feelings can so easily be very hurt.

Much of what Tom says cannot be verified and remains anecdotal.

slung limbs

Sebastian had this thing: he could not sleep with another. He was used to being the master of his own domain, as it were; the mattress was his and his alone, and he had trouble actually sleeping with another man in his bed. There was simply not enough room. Plus: it was too distracting. A squirming, snorting, 185-pound unknown entity was impossible to ignore.

And what could not be ignored, could not be slept with.

And if he wasn't ignoring, but exploring, the 185-pound squirming entity, well, that was not exactly sleeping either. That was the activity referred to as sleeping together which does not involve any actual sleep.

In his own bed, he had not actually slept with another, certainly not for very long. Sleeping itself had never been a featured activity when he had hosted that rare beast: an overnight guest. Usually, there was too much to talk about, and not just from the world of insects.

Maybe eventually, sleep would have arrived on the tail of sheer exhaustion, but sadly things never went that far.

☉

Sometimes, Sebastian thinks, that is the whole thing with Tom, the thing that made it all work. The thing that it is all about. It all boiled down to this one thing: he slept with Tom. He slept well with Tom. He curled up with Tom and if he was tired, he went right to sleep. Just like that.

☉

Sleeping together became both a metaphor (for greater and lesser intimacies) and the ultimate literal truth. The act of sleeping together, cuddled in a heap, spooning back to front, a hairy forearm at home on a chest: this is what they did. This is how they defined themselves. This is what they were. They were affectionate men, but more than that, they were lovers, they were in a relationship, they were special friends. They slept together.

So many other things were undone, or offset, because they slept together so well. Sleeping together made everything possible.

That is, when it worked.

When limbs were slung with abandon, and in a strange way, not even noticed, which is what made the limb-slinging so special: it was perfectly normal. And could be ignored.

It was perfectly normal to sling a limb over the man sleeping next to you.

And go back to sleep.

a man of the world in the world of men

Tom has his spiritual pursuits. Tom's spiritual perambulations provide access to sensitive young confused types open to some vigorous mentoring. Like moths, they flock to the light, arriving in fluttery waves. Tom only has to reach out to grab one as it flutters by, looking lost and a little wounded.

Confusion leads to experimentation, and a surprising number of boys who say "Oh, I've never done that before," take to it like birds to the air. The ass of boys, Tom considered, was finely made for fucking, and many a boy who says he has "never done that" knows in his blackest heart how to offer it up. Faces clenched in exquisite agony.

Tom likes their clenched faces, their gritted jaws. The whole furrowed puppy look. It is all about the face. Tom studies the face, charting each ripple and tremor, as he works his way inside.

Tom likes a manboy who has never been fucked before. These boys were ripe without knowing they were ripe (or at least, pretended not to know). Tom found this incredibly sexy. Tom likes believing the boy is virtually innocent, and is eager to experience the tension until discovering he may have been wrong.

What is most exciting for Tom is when the boy is wavering, and things could go either way. Sometimes it ends up being an act of gratitude, sometimes an act of depravity. Sometimes it is horniness, or curiosity, sometimes both, a powerful, powerful combo.[12]

Curiosity and lust have struck the truth from many statements which went, "I've never done that before."

And as the story goes, the boys were bi-curious, and Tom was bi. The match was made. Curiosity took the bait it was looking for.

And the rest just happened.

You can't fuck innocence, Tom says. And you can't fuck a face. No, not really.

But you can watch the face and see everything. You can see the innocence being fucked. You can see the fucking in the face.

The thought of an ass that has never been fucked before drives Tom insane. A slightly baffled expression consolidates Tom's bone. Looking like maybe having second thoughts about the whole experimental process is enough to send Tom right to the very edge. He will stop and hover, staring at the boy's face, not daring to move. It is the edge of knowing he will never be there again. Never be in this exact place ever again. It is the

---

[12] Curiosity and Lust are joined together in a kind of same-sex union. See also Confusion, linked to Experimentation in a marriage of convenience.

cutting edge of impermanence, and Tom managed to combine this spiritual truth with his repetitive pursuit of fresh boys. And sees no contradiction. Everything, as he says, is consensual, and everything is transitory.

Except impermanence. Impermanence, apparently, is here to stay.

pillow talk

Certain experiences in the life of Tom are lumped together in the category "laid with alcohol." These are not stories Tom is quick to tell, he asserts, before rehashing one or two.

An LWA is a pocket of insanity which used to envelop Tom with some regularity. Apparently he is over that now. Now he explores his power issues through meditation instead of through seduction. He claims power instead of displaying power. He owns his power, Tom explains, instead of whatever the Sanskrit word is for when possessions own you. There is probably not a specific word for that, since the world was not so "made anxious through consumer expectations" back when Sanskrit was sweeping the charts.

So there was this one guy, an LWA of course, so sweet and innocent and adorable, who let Tom do anything. If it came out of Tom's cock, he wanted it, on him, in him, all over him. Nothing fazed him. He sprawled sweetly in the bathtub and dared Tom to just do it. The more

Tom showered him and spunked him up, the more he wanted. Tom came inside him, because the guy wanted it, and at the time, it was kind of hot to do it. Tom wanted to nail a guy, and come inside him, but would never express this.

This had never really happened before. Not so much.

Tom, you see, was not harsh. Tom was not a big harsh gay fag, no, he was just into fucking cute guys and doing whatever he could get away with. But not a fag. Not really.

With this bottomless bottom boy, Tom got away with a lot. And that created its own excitement. Enough so that Tom still talks about it, still gets off on it.

Still tells the story to get things worked up and underway.

Why do you think Sebastian keeps hearing it? Even though Tom says some of these stories are things he is not proud of, he keeps talking about them.

Tom fucked the unfazed boy, just like that, without even naming such a thing; it was just fucking. Fucking is what it was, that's all it was, just fucking, but Tom still talks of that boy, who really he didn't much care for at the time. This boy stirs him still, and yet when they overlapped as much as they ever did, when they occupied the same space, it was obvious this was not to last. Nor would Tom want it to. He couldn't wait to get out of there. This was not for the best. Even as he screwed the kid, Tom couldn't wait to get out of there and on his way.

And yet he lingers. He still has not let it go. Still revisits moments which could not last.

Still tells the story of this boy, laid with alcohol, of course, who let him do anything.

Tom tells this story, opening himself up, as Sebastian works his way inside. Tom's face says something complicated about the uncared-for boy.

Tom was bi-curious and into guys who were not necessarily fags. Tom was put off somehow by full-blown fags. Tom liked a bit of tension. It was more exciting not to know what was going to happen than to have a guy drooling all over you. Tom liked nice, shy boys, especially athletic, nice, shy boys.

Lots of sensitive, spiritual guys are bi-curious. It's part of their openness and commitment to personal exploration. The special thing about curiosity is that no matter what it never goes away. Guys can be curious, and dabbling, and be sensitive all over the place and even have a sequence of male lovers ("spiritual friends"), and yet end up just as bi-curious as ever.[13]

---

[13] The difference between "bi-curious" and "bisexual" has never been satisfactorily explained to Sebastian.

Tom had originally even gone to this group, called the Telepathic Matrix, rumoured to be fantastic, not for the guided meditation, but because he knew sensitive guys are into other sensitive guys.[14]

Tom figured at least he'd pick up the jargon.

The Telepathic Matrix was a hotbed of sensitivity, then it kind of petered out and Tom stopped going. He needed to take a break anyway as it turns out because he was gearing up to join the cult. After all, he already spoke the language.

---

[14] Actually, Tom said, "Sensitive guys like to get fucked hard," but one suspects this statement is not meant to be taken literally.

skillful means

Today, Tom decided he wanted to fuck the blond boy.
The one he wasn't sure about. He'd seen the boy many
times, and talked to him, and wondered about his
accent (Saskatchewan). Thinking about him now, about
the fit of his jeans around his hips, the roll in his stride,
the smirk in his smile, the blue gaze flickering under
the curve of the low-pulled beak, Tom felt a stirring,
and in that stirring was the realization that he wanted to
fuck that blond boy.

And so the crush crushed along, another whirl
of another crush. The crush quieted Tom's mind, as
it provided a focus. The crush became his centre, his
point of mindfulness. He embraced his obsession,
his attachment, as a point of mindfulness. He loved
spirituality for its flexibility. Skillful means was a
delight. Skillful means was anything you wanted it to
be, and Tom was thrilled that the blond boy and his
desire to fuck the blond boy could become a point of
mindfulness.

Without a crush, Tom didn't know what to think
about, or rather, what to be aware of not thinking about.
Without a crush, the second attention had no point of
focus, no moment of liberation. Not thinking about the

crush became the expression of freedom, of space, of overcoming attachments and aversions. It was ironic, but there it was. Tom needed a crush in order to be free.

Tom's crushes were practical. A crush was a new reason to live, motivation to make plans and do things. Crushes were efficient, for Tom. They were, above all, practical. No fantasy crushes for Tom. If Tom were to have a crush, it had to be an actual person in his life who he got along with (or who was at least attractive) and who had flirted with him (or at least was attractive). Maybe they'd already even made out some. That's what it took for Tom to have a crush.

This criteria includes so many people.

He also had guys lined up as possible crushes, and that is what this blond boy was. A possible crush. Just waiting to happen. Possibly.

A crush for Tom was not an accident or a surprise. They never took him by surprise because he saw them coming everywhere. There were dozens of potential crushes lined up circling in Tom's consciousness like jetliners in a holding pattern at a busy international airport awaiting permission to land. Flocks of them, and either they landed efficiently or crashed and burned unnoticed, or perhaps flew on to an alternative destination.

Throughout the turmoil of arrivals and departures, Tom claimed he just went with the flow.

The flow really is what he is, not what he goes with.

The flow is what goes past him, saturating his consciousness.

Now the flow is all about a blond boy, and the space around the blond boy which is also not the blond boy, but is more than the blond boy and contains him. Like his jeans, which hide and display and define and conceal and announce. His jeans are not the blond boy, but they catch the eye and frame precarious desire. Tom seeks the space in his mindfulness which is not the blond boy and is the blond boy.

Blond is a softer look, so already a blond boy is a little femmy. When did blond femmy boys become so hot? Tom in his thirties is noticing femmy boys like he never did before. Twinks look soft and pretty. Boys now look softer. A blond boy or a blonde girl, an outdoorsy kind of blonde girl, or behind-closed-doors kind of boy, doesn't matter so much. One of Tom's fantasies, which he no longer indulges, was a three-way with two blonds, a brother and a sister, the brother gay of course, so brother and sister both want Tom, they want him, and he fucks them both. Tom has beat off so many times with this fantasy, being wanted by both the blond brother and the blonde sister, and fucking them both, one after the other.

Now as he quiets his mind, traces of his fantasy resurface and mingle with the smirk in the smile of the blond boy, the one he wonders about today.

With the way blond boys look today, Tom no longer thinks about their sisters. The sister, initially, had been the point of entry into the fantasy, leading up to the brother, and has brought Tom along to this moment, to this blond boy who effortlessly flaunts a subdued paradoxical sexiness.

Skillful means penetrating the paradox.

The crush is not about sex, Tom says. The crush is about being alive.

the difference between the species

Tom in his words is bisexual, bi-curious, straight, and straight-acting.

This meant that Tom, technically, does not have gaydar.

Disqualified on the grounds that he was not, in fact, gay.

Therefore, no gaydar.

What he has instead is being bi-curious, which more than makes up for any lack of gaydar. Bi-curious takes Tom far. Sebastian's gaydar has never been reliable (he does not use the word "buggy" in this context). Whatever Tom has instead of gaydar is definitely more finely calibrated, and as fully functional as Data ever was on those *Next Generation* episodes where the android had sex.

Now that it was on his mind, Sebastian wondered if

perhaps he was bi-curious. He, Sebastian, not the android.

He was curious about bisexuality. Very curious about particular bisexual men. If bi-curious meant being curious about bisexuality then Sebastian was indeed very bi-curious.

Sebastian was not curious about whether he himself was bisexual. He was certain he was gay, but started thinking there was no real reason he could not say he was bisexual. There were no performance standards. It was all about self-identification.

Tom said that bisexual was the new gay. Bisexual is what young guys say they are even if they only sleep with other guys.

∽

Sebastian has formed the opinion that bisexual men became mostly gay, based on an admittedly informal survey of mating habits. Bisexual men often make out with each other, using a shared attraction for women as sex-talk to get going. This veneer of straight-acting, so thin as to be virtually transparent, is one of those impenetrable ironies that bisexual men seem to attract into their lives.

Gay men, on the other hand, universally believe that "bisexual" is just a phase in the proud, joyous, one-way journey towards complete self-acceptance and being gay gay GAY! One hundred percent gay.

Tom did not agree. It was not a phase and it was

not ironic. He was bisexual and that was only a phase to the extent that his life was a phase. Tom claimed that guys did not go through any process of starting out bi and then realizing they are gay. What happens, Tom explained, is that bi guys find it easier to hook up with other guys. They start to seem gay, because of that. They're always with guys, but they're still bisexual. They're basically just lazy men; women are more work.

To the untrained eye, Tom said, lazy bisexuals may appear to be gay. But they're still bisexual.

Research must continue. Lazy bisexual has a whiff of left-handed Buddhism about it, and Sebastian has vowed not to fall so easily for these things.

Part 4

AWARENESS

The Sanskrit word for awareness is *smriti* which means "recognition," "recollection." Recollection not in the sense of remembering the past but in the sense of recognizing the product of mindfulness.... Having experienced the precision of mindfulness, we might ask the question of ourselves, "What should I do with that? What can I do next?" And awareness reassures us that we do not really have to do anything with it but can leave it in its own natural place.... So awareness is the willingness not to cling to the discoveries of mindfulness, and mindfulness is just precision; things are what they are.

– Chögyam Trungpa, *The Myth of Freedom, and the Way of Meditation*

living hell

Each person, Tom says, is an outpost of consciousness.
And consciousness begins with awareness.

What Tom seems to be saying is that there is
ordinary mind, and that is where most of us dwell
with our suffering, stuck in a living hell of our own
concoction with our hatred, and greed, and envy and
bitterness, feeling all the pain and torment of emotional
obsession.

The need to rant and rage: that is ordinary mind.

But there is something beyond ordinary mind.

Something much more vast.

And the first small step in a vast journey is
awareness. Awareness of how the mind works to trap us.
Awareness of what we do in our heads is the first step
towards seeing our ordinary mind. And seeing beyond.

Sebastian began with becoming very aware of how Tom
had trapped *him*.

Sebastian became very aware of how Tom in his
quiet way used his spirituality to manipulate the hell
out of everyone around him.

This fruit of awareness was not to Tom's taste.

The permutations on the topic became their own temporary living hell and need not be recorded. One now has clearer boundaries. Suffice it to say, the pursuit of awareness remains a challenge to all concerned.

flirting with omniscience

Tom's spiritual pursuits may have hinted at flakiness, but did not scream alarm.

When they first met, Tom was exploring. A course in power yoga in an overheated room, a weekend on shamanism in the modern world, books on auras and chakras. Tom had formed an oddly firm belief in reincarnation. He occasionally dropped in for vipassana meditation with Tibetan Buddhists.

Somewhere along the line, he'd hooked up with people who were part of the Centre and participated in an anger workshop and watched a video called *Bodhisattva and Beyond*. Then every Friday night, Tom regularly attended what was called the Abun-Dance. This was an unabashedly pagan ritual with drums and chanting, meditation cycles, and group confessions, followed by freestyle interpretive dancing which could break out into expressive seizures, on a good night perhaps even with accompanying glossolalia. Dancers were "witnessed" by a chanting, clapping circle, and the performance could evolve into a form of contact improv, which was exhilarating when it went well: just like the excitement and flow of anything which goes so well you don't notice it happening, until suddenly you do notice and then it stops. That's what contact improv can be like. You have to let yourself go and step into the moment. According to Tom.

Sebastian went once. The moment, as it turned out, was not for him to step into uncritically.

He went because Tom asked him to, and felt awkward the whole time. Sebastian saw how the elements could be cathartic for those inclined towards the histrionic, but was suspicious of the structure supporting the open-weave fabric of the disorienting chaos. The hidden structure was tight-laced, like a foundation garment. The group claimed to be offering freedom, but was actually selling something else. They talked freedom, but took it away. They talked freedom, but sold constraints. His discomfort, Sebastian decided later, had actually been a valid, almost instinctive reaction to covert manipulation.

The confession segment of the Abun-Dance was a means to let go, to empty out, providing space for the "abundance" to flow. Sebastian was shocked to hear a glowing-faced young woman speak almost casually about being raped. She still blamed herself, maybe even had invited it, and questioned the way she expressed her inner conflicts. The next confessor, admirably candid, spoke of the crippling shame he lived with from deceiving his partner, having an affair behind her back.

Only much later, after quietly cross-classifying slices of information gleaned from Tom, did Sebastian confirm that these two confessors were plants. The word "rape" had been oddly turquoise when uttered, but the accuracy of Sebastian's emotional chromometer, such as it is, was highly variable, especially in crowds. A tinge of turquoise was not that remarkable under the conditions.

Even Tom felt moved to note that the couple displayed the blatant contradiction of an ambitious spirituality. These two were clearly power-behind-the-throne wannabes, and placed their faith in the belief that recruitment services would be rewarded. Their roles were rehearsed and calculated to get the evening moving, open everything up, establish the "high bar" of confession. Drama was more compelling than a misguided and small-minded reliance on accuracy.

The glowing-faced girl, who looked as if she were made of pure sunshine, was in fact the very partner deceived by her two-faced, shame-based husband. The rape may have been metaphorical: high bar confessors channeled permission to just make things up. They had creative, flexible identities: tending to the symbolic, emblematic of problems that did happen to actual people the world over.

This sort of cheerful, straightforward duplicity confounded Sebastian. The truth was so much stranger than fiction that Sebastian saw no need to make anything up.

The truth was always strange enough.

∞

Looking back, Sebastian can see a definite shift in

Tom's attitude after the Kardapa Lampa breezed through town on his nomadic mission.

"When I met the Kardapa Lampa" became a phrase often heard from Tom. Sebastian could see how Tom had created a certain category of thing to be reached for at critical moments, a kind of spiritual touchstone with smooth, familiar edges for Tom to handle and present as evidence, as validation, as a link to something bigger, more substantial, more real, a link in effect in the chain of credentials.

Meeting the Kardapa Lampa had been Tom's moment in some kind of spotlight, not unlike other people when they meet the Dalai Lama and who are, from that point on, full of stories about when they met the Dalai Lama.

But this obviously was not the Dalai Lama, and that's why it seemed to Sebastian that Tom was missing something here.

Sebastian wondered why Tom needed such a thing. And if so, why such a small thing.

Tom was so beyond dualism that, with his advanced dyslexia, he could miss the point and not even notice.

A good workshop on personal awareness is what Tom needed, not what he should have been selling. How to make Tom become aware that the workshop is happening all around him?

When Tom met the Kardapa Lampa, he glowed for

days. ("Start where you are," the Kardapa Lampa
had told Tom, who had with uncharacteristic false
modesty doubted his ability to absorb the essence of the
teachings.)

The Kardapa Lampa had a seemingly effortless,
unforced charisma, and this was enough apparently to
avoid being labelled as just another smiling windbag
with the gift of gab who in the charlatan tradition had
adopted an airy-fairy teaching name and travelled the
world selling simple wisdom.

Except the Kardapa Lampa was the real thing,
according to Tom.

The name, though, was not a real name. The name
was a title.

The Kardapa Lampa was both a reincarnating
lineage, and a theory Tom ascribed to. The current title
holder had been empowered through a series of events
whose legitimacy provoked controversy and much
bitter debate. People loved him or they hated him. The
Kardapa Lampa was either tearing Buddhism apart, or
he was a living embodiment of the teachings.

There was no middle way here.

Sebastian teased Tom about his flakier edges, because
it was easy to do. It was the sort of teasing which gave
them something in common. They each had a position
to take and the banter became routine.

Sebastian actually took pleasure in Tom's spiritual

pursuits. It confirmed something for Sebastian. It meant he had a spiritual side too. This, to Sebastian, was fascinating information, but he had no idea what to do with it.

He was spiritual. Okay, so what?

Sebastian had heard love was blind, so he couldn't be sure if what he saw or knew was really so. His impressions might be fueled by the hallucinations which love is known to produce. He so obviously hallucinated around Tom. At times he imagined Tom to have almost supernatural abilities: he was that special, that gifted, and that was why Sebastian felt so overwhelmingly infatuated, so swamped with feeling. If he tried to convey these feelings to Tom, it sounded trite: "You have a lot of potential." It never came out right. The hallucination collapsed, he felt let down and deluded, and that's how he knew it was only a hallucination in the first place and not something more real, like a memory.

They always say love is blind, but maybe memory can be blind too, the kind of blindness where you can only see the thing you want to see. Sebastian could look at Tom and see more than there was there, and this was either a form of optimistic self-deceit or a kind of hope. Is hope delusional?

Or we could say love is blind but not totally blind. Love can still see some shadows, and changes in the light. Love is blind but can still see shadows.

This is not how one normally speaks, according to the literature, while still in love. In any event, it was a challenge to let Tom be Tom, and to let go of expectations Tom could never live up to. The challenge was to see Tom as Tom was.

Sebastian thought, but could not be sure, that Tom was wasting his spiritual capital on that tantric mind control prosperity cult. Was this feeling a kind of pride reflected in Tom, his peer-companion and mirror-friend?

He is mine, Sebastian wanted to scream. My lover! Mine!

Tom's involvement with the cult seemed a contradiction. He was wasting his time there. Tom prayed for the enlightenment of all sentient beings, yet hid his own light under the cult's bushel. Was this really Tom's best expression?

For reasons that Sebastian could not articulate, he felt that Tom's metamorphosis was incomplete.

Or else he was just confused.

Obvious matters confused Sebastian, or at least, he found it confusing how others could overlook the most simple, obvious matters. People were supposedly sentient, and yet they needed so much help to see the light, even when it was shining directly on them. Even shining right on their naked faces, people need to be told, open your eyes and see the light.

It's all about seeing the mind, Tom says. That is
the embedded Buddhist teaching in mind training.
Awareness of the mind is the first step towards realizing
all is mind.

Ego is mind.

Tom talked about ego so much. Everything was
ego. A vast quantity of ego was available for eradication.
Sebastian could not understand Tom's acceptance of
the pervasiveness of ego, which persisted despite all
efforts. Sebastian didn't know if *this* was ego, thinking
that he knew better than Tom what was good for Tom.

Sebastian did know that he enjoyed good solid
dualistic moments. It thrilled him to have a strong clear
opinion: Tom, good; cult, bad.

It was so much more satisfying than: pride, iffy;
ego, persistent and unstoppable.

Confusion, unclear.

Tom claimed there was so much irony here (which
Sebastian could only intellectualize). Irony was a kind
of backwards humour, so Sebastian wondered if a taste
for irony was part of Tom's dyslexia. Only seeing other
people's irony. Never looking backwards at your own
missteps.

Due to Tom's easy-going, sensitive nature, things
had gone this far. It was Tom's open, spiritual side
which had laid the trap that Tom found and then
walked right into. He was a searcher, and so he
searched for this and found it.

In any event, Sebastian felt that it would be Tom's
spirituality, his questing nature, which has taken him

this far, and would in turn lead him through this.

Perversely, Sebastian had great faith in Tom's spirituality.

And what Tom's spirituality required right now, Sebatian decided, was a spiritual friend.

A true one.

Whatever that meant.

noticed noticing

Sebastian noted, as a child, that other children avoided him. If he sidled up to them they skittered away. It was not always obvious, but it happened.

Whenever he opened his mouth to say anything, children fled.

Even so, Sebastian carries with him what might be called the reek of desperation. This reek is not chemical but emotional or spiritual, and can be readily perceived by those equipped with whatever remote-sensing apparatus is required to detect the apparent reek of desperation.

Perhaps just eyes, but what is it that they see?

Sebastian does not know how people perceive the blanket of awkwardness he keeps tripping over. Does it glow?

(When stuck inside a strong blind exterior, his head swells and he goes anosmic. "Anosmic" means nose-blind, and even when Sebastian goes nose-blind he can still smell a little bit. He smells the shadows. Sebastian has never been completely anosmic and cannot imagine what that must be like.)

Sebastian's strategy, as a social reject child, was to attempt to befriend another outcast boy in their cohort. Incredibly, even another social outcast preferred to reject him rather than risk being tainted by the reek of desperation Sebastian so obviously emanated.

As long as he could remember, Sebastian had been programmed to expect that being a man was enough for all it would be called upon to hold. Being a man could contain any situation.

This is how Sebastian put up with everyone hating him. They called him Bugboy but inside he was Bugman, protected by a strong external skeleton. Sebastian lived inside Bugman, and that is how he put up with being called spaz and Spaz-tian and stupid Bug-Eyes. Told he belonged in the Bughouse. He put up with being rejected by the social outcast who was scared of being tainted. He put up with everything by living deep within the Bugman exterior skeleton, and not showing a thing.

But then something entirely new slid up next to Sebastian following the metamorphosis, marked by hair, that signaled a developmental plateau.

This new thing was like a riddle which gave itself to the gangly young Sebastian so slowly that he did not even notice at first solving the eye-sliding mystery. Did not notice finding all the clues. The answer to the riddle was shy, quiet, and barely noticed. Yet studied, ever so carefully and quietly. Strictly a kind of wispy fantasy, in its beginning. The fantasy was practically unconscious, it was so tentative.

And yet it was there. And it was, at first, no more than an armpit.

This armpit grew on him.

One day, late in the school year it would have been, when the first heat of the season struck hard and the earth smelled like summer, this almost unconscious fantasy of Sebastian's became real with a jolt. As real as noticing all of a sudden that a quiet boy at school was actually the most compelling thing in the universe. A quiet boy who smelled like cinnamon and something burnt, but not toast.

Sebastian found himself hoping.

Hoping this boy in his sleeveless top would lift his arm for some reason, to stretch or to scratch his head. He never asked questions, but please would he somehow flash the pale underbelly framing a bushy patch of dampened tendrils.

Burnt, like wooden matches, but not cigarettes. Cinnamon and wood smoke. A suggestion of dusty lilac.

There was so much to hope for, and this is what Sebastian noticed. He noticed hoping the boy would yawn and stretch both arms up, lace his fingers behind his head, and leisurely give the full display. Flashing the twins. Sebastian hoped he would see this, see more, see all of it, see everything there was to see of this quiet boy who had so captured him.

The armpit was the first thing Sebastian noticed noticing. Boys, yes. Delicate, vulnerable, and manly, the fantasy was fantastic, but had become much more real. As real as clumping tufts in a pit of soft pale silk. As real as noticing a quiet boy. As real as hoping to glimpse the pale arm crotch of this quiet boy. Skin, and hair, peeking out. The intersection of so much, bristling.

Bristling like hope.

Fantasy slid over into reality. They had been walking alongside each other all along. Sebastian's world immediately overflowed with gangly, sharp-featured, clear-eyed boys as sleek and beautiful as spotty hawks. They preened and swooped, and were dangerous up close. They were almost painful to look at.

"And they still are," Sebastian said.

the means of awareness

Awareness means paying attention.

Awareness means seeing.

Awareness means being aware that what you believe to be true is just that, a belief. A construction of the mind. Truth is always there too, more truth. The truth behind the belief. Or in spite of the belief. Or inspired by the belief. The belief and the truth never entirely escape each other.

The Sanskrit word for awareness is *smriti*, which no one can pronounce. This may explain why awareness has not become as well-known in the west as karma, dharma, and nirvana.

Awareness means being willing to see past what you have already seen before. Awareness has fresh eyes. Awareness means being able to see the world around you, and to keep seeing the world around you.

Awareness is a constant meditation on things and the names of things.

future in sects

Sebastian feels guilty calling it a cult and yet persists in doing so.

He feels guilty because he had agreed to Tom's request that he not call it a cult, and yet he still does, except not when Tom can hear.

It is a complex topic. Sebastian has done research, and yet he does not really feel he knows what genuine spirituality is, or if he'd recognize it if it reared up and bit him in the face.

Sebastian has doubts that he is actually even qualified to determine whether a spiritual group is genuine or perhaps a bit cultish. And yet in this situation Sebastian has made his judgment. He has decided and so he insists on calling it a cult. At least to himself. Because that is what it is.

He would like to say, does the truth hurt Tom? Why can't I call it a cult? Why is Tom so sensitive about one little four-letter word? He seems very attached to the word in the way that aversion is attachment, the very thing his group actually preaches about, warns about.

Attachments, aversions, and ego. Tom bristles at the hint of an accusation or a comment, bristling like a cock confronted with a mirror. Inflamed at the sight of something just like him.

Tom's denial display spoke of much.

But what?

Sometimes Sebastian thought that Tom's denial around the cult was because of, well, convenience. The group attracted young people in search of themselves, in search of meaning, and in finding their way through the teachings discover Tom's willingness to accommodate sensitive young men who were beautiful and questioning, spiritual young men ripe for initiation, infatuation, and indulgence: the holy trinity of spiritual transcendence in the physical plane.

Tom held each one of these boys and granted them an opportunity to pour out their hearts and souls, listening as if he had never heard such a compelling story, and would even cry with the boy if that's what it took to get laid. Tom dove right in there for the duration, and that is why each boy came out ahead. They shared whatever most needed to be honoured and acknowledged, and Tom listened and went on a journey with each of them, with all of them, all their different journeys.

The group made this possible in a way.

The group was not gay, but sensitive boys are naturally bi-curious.

So Tom would miss this pool of talent in which he fished for enlightenment and hooked up with manboys.

Of course, there was more to it than that.
Or so Tom claimed. More than a little indignant.

∞

Sebastian has reached an accommodation with himself.
The future involves the cult in the same way that
the future involves things which cannot be foreseen,
ignored, forgotten, or dismissed.

Tom might wake up to the cult, or else Sebastian's
opinion might change.

Awareness means recognizing that there may be
things you are just going to have to overlook.

being in your shoulders

Awareness means reaching out with understanding.

Which is exactly what Sebastian was trying to do. Sebastian tried to reach out to Tom's world. The touchy, feely, New Age world Tom inhabited.

The class was called yoga, but it was not yoga, which means union.

This class was not about union.

This is where the warp of Sebastian's understanding does not mesh with the reconstruction of others in the fabric of events. Sebastian can only be expected to do so much in the quest for understanding. There is only so far Sebastian can go on his own. One will soon see what an absurd challenge this yoga class turned out to be, and how although it provided a glimpse into Tom's world it also illustrated many areas of difference. Did it bring them closer?

Confusion loomed throughout existence. There was some red.

Sebastian can never hear names because he cannot see and listen at the same time. He cannot look at a person's face if they are speaking. A smiling man wearing a bandana over his shaved skull, multi-syllable name, appeared fiercely relaxed. Explained the fundamental point of all that we are doing. The bandana had faded mauve paisleys. The class leaned in, held a collective breath … about to be spoon-fed a morsel of yogic wisdom in one sound bite.

"The whole point is, this is an exercise of being in your shoulders."

What? Sebastian recoiled.

No, this was an exercise in not laughing out loud, which Sebastian dared not do. Mr. Fiercely Relaxed probably had feelings (he looked the type). Which came first, do you suppose: the issues, or the fierce need to relax?

Sebastian was trying very hard to genuinely take this seriously. It should not be necessary to have to point that out.

And even though some people say that Sebastian doesn't feel things quite the same way as you and I do, what do people know, anyway. People can say what they want, but Sebastian feels a whole lot of things.

And one thing Sebastian felt quite strongly about is that his mind is in his head, and not in his shoulders.

And so Sebastian remained in his "head" where traditionally the mind is ascribed to reside. Sebastian could not be in his shoulders. Sebastian could not simply let his arms drift up up up to the ceiling as he relaxed and exhaled all tension in his upper back, his spine and his arms and shoulders. Imagine your arms are weightless! Come on, do it! Weightless! Now!

Imagination only went so far. Sebastian's arms weighed twelve and a half pounds each. Approximately.

That was not weightless. Now, or then.

Sebastian started laughing because he simply had to. Then he managed to stop laughing, but still needed to chat a bit with other yoga students out of nervousness. They were right there, and not talking to anyone else. Of course Sebastian stayed on topic. It wasn't like he started talking about a movie or the scent gland secretions of water beetles used to flavour salt in Japan. He asked strictly yoga-related questions, like, Do you think I'm doing this right? You look very flexible. Are you, um, really flexible?

The yoga teacher said to everyone in a voice of gentle guidance, "No need to talk," and then directly to Sebastian, "You can ask me questions."

Well, the obvious first question was, what exactly did he mean? Talk or not?

Sebastian stifled his urge to press for clarification. For example, did questions have to be yoga-related? Because Sebastian was always willing to ask Did you know? questions about bat bugs. (Did you know the bat bug is a bloodsucking ectoparasite closely related to bed bugs? Did you know bat bugs will feed on humans? Did you know that very little is actually known about bat bugs?)

All the fiercely relaxed instructor probably meant was, be quiet and relax, but because Sebastian at the time felt unable to clarify the conflicting instructions, immediately there arose a barrier between Sebastian and his free pursuit of the benefits of this yoga class. The issue was, what do you pay attention to? What do you believe? Which thing that is said do you believe?

But these were the exact questions which could not be answered.

So, it may not be that well-known, but yes, people have been invited to leave an introductory yoga class in this country.

the campaign for bug juice awareness

Research has shown that someone eating, for example, chocolate-covered raisins, may not wish to take a moment to learn and appreciate what it is that makes their tasty treat so shiny.

Each precious little morsel glistening with the shininess of life, preserved with a glaze.

What is it coated with, do you suppose?

Confectioner's shellac, it's called, or resinous glaze.

An edible shellac.

This paragraph explains where the concept of shellac was born. The glossy secretion of a scale-type insect was much admired for its hard, protective sheen. These insects are called "lac," from the Sanskrit for a very large number. The hunger and lust for such slick shininess in the world was so severe that soon these insects went from being agricultural pests to being cultivated on huge plantations in cheap, lush countries. And thus, shellac. Made from lac.

And so to this day we have lac farms, millions and

millions of lac living and dying so that your chocolate-covered raisin or peanut glistens.

Originally, this glossy secretion protected the insect. Now the scale insects are harvested and sacrificed so their secretions can coat chocolate.[15] The shellac keeps your candy treat all neat and shiny and delicious-looking.

Protected and tantalizing.

Totally covered in the most attractive bug juice.

Another scale insect is the traditional source of dyes such as carminic acid, i.e., carmine. It takes 70,000 cochineal insects to make a pound of dye. Used in food and cosmetics. For example, do you know what is in your red lipstick? Yes, bug juice makes you pretty.

The campaign for awareness will help you appreciate the contributions insects make. See that red stripe on a stick of fake crab? Thank you, scale insects, for your food-grade dye.[16]

---

[15] Chocolate itself is made possible by cocoa plants being fertilized by tiny midges (a type of fly).

[16] The joke entomologists always tell is, How do you describe the life cycle of the cochineal scale insect?: Living and dyeing.

developmental plateaus

Sebastian has been pegged on many developmental plateaus. They are at best temporary destinations.

He does not care what someone decides about him. It does not matter, he does not care, he has to work to imagine another person even has feelings. What does it matter to Sebastian what someone thinks about him?

He does not care and so he is free.

Free to acknowledge that he is at a developmental plateau right now.

He is at a developmental plateau, and Tom is at his developmental plateau, and the manboys all have a developmental plateau on their own planet, and that is where they know each other from.

Seriously, we all have developmental plateaus. But whether these plateaus are staggered, or tiered, in series or in parallel, or whether one is better: that is another matter.

They are different, but equal in aspiration.

Different, but equal.

Different but equal does not translate into good or bad.

Different, but equal, is just that.

Equal, but different. Differently equal.

Sebastian is learning to watch for colours that match the words.

He has become a much better listener, and there is still opportunity for improvement.

Sebastian can learn more now by keeping still than by asking questions. People tell him more if he doesn't ask questions. Tom tells him more.

Besides listening, Sebastian is learning to wait and watch. Watch what happens when the weight of the words was released from the body through the voice.

In the sense that Sebastian feels others deserve praise for their efforts and accomplishments, it could be acknowledged that Sebastian deserves some credit for the developmental plateaus he has taken in stride and left in his dust.

The thing is, people can learn.

People can learn to become something they would not have imagined possible. No matter what, people can still learn more.

The best thing about plateaus is that there is lots of room to camp.

And they can be made to feel like home.

the colour of emotions

Sebastian has become increasingly aware of the correlation between his sensational experience of colours, and emotions flowing in the vicinity.

Blue and green mean different things, but at any given moment it can be impossible to draw the line between hope and envy. Green obviously means growth, but can encompass a desire for conquest, or overgrowth, or obliteration. Growth, and the need to overwhelm the competition, are attributes of green vigour.

Blue is for things that may or may not exist, like hope and desire.

Red flares up and means passion, anger, lust. Solid, supportive passions are never red, but may be tinged with pink or rose.

Red, Sebastian realizes, is a colour he tries not to see. Red scares Sebastian. Red floods in from the edges and blocks out everything else. Blocks out reason, blocks out sanity, and interrupts awareness and even memory. Red blocks out everything except red.

The red times which most scared Sebastian need not be gone into here. Suffice it to say that red has become established as the colour of crisis, and a flag warning of bad judgment all around.

Red needs to be paid attention to, but also should not be taken too seriously.

The red times came like a tide of turbulence when Sebastian was a teenager. This was also a time when Sebastian's mother, who is not a feature of this exposition, became very disillusioned with her lot in life. She became largely inert and stayed in bed. Sebastian would glance in the bedroom as he passed, and note whether the lump had moved. Wrapped in blankets, his mother lay in the fetal position, curled in on herself in a cocoon of unknown duration.

Sebastian noted the condition of the lump in the bed, just as he noted the lines of red ants circumnavigating the kitchen island and the silverfish darting in the shoals of the pantry.

The lump in the bed slept while he was about. They lived separate lives, and only intersected where foraging overlapped. Sebastian had taken over some chores years ago, and now just did more. He had become quite particular in his routines, and it was easier to do things his way. He needed to clean things himself to know that it was done. He was very particular.

Periodically cocoon mummy stirred. In the middle of the night, she cooked. In the morning, there was food. Sebastian would eat and clean and freeze leftovers, neatly labelled. The next night, she would cook again. Each month or so, she would cook several nights in a row, finishing each cycle with a white night of dessert-baking. The smell of chocolate chip cookies was excruciating.

∽

When Sebastian was much younger, they'd had a different relationship. For years, he hung on every word that came out of her mouth. Asked endless questions just to keep her going. Yellow was his overwhelmingly favourite colour. Yellow was like the sun and the touch of her warm hand and the yolk full of nourishment. He bathed in the warm yellow of her words.

Couldn't get enough of the sound of her voice. Sebastian awash in a sea of bright yellow, like a sunflower, turning his face to the light.

After puberty, Sebastian began to voice doubts at particular elements of received wisdom. He started to question authority. He became difficult to handle. He started to second guess her decisions in life. The experience of yellow had faded to a uniform beige. He was frank and honest, and coming from a fourteen-year-old, seemed dismissive. Rebellion is a harsh judge. Sebastian no longer even tried to be polite to his mother. He had no patience for the froth sloshing out from the busy churnings of her mind. Sebastian tuned her out (and tuned into other networks: the world of men, especially the gay world, and international entomology). Sebastian's mother slowly wound down unnoticed, until she lay there wrapped in blankets, swaddled in the indifference which permeated her being.

Sebastian noticed, of course. He observed.

A pupating lump in the bed. Fetal position. Metamorphosis was intermittent, and predictable as seasons.

A lump in the bed who sometimes cooked in the dead of night, filling the house with the smell of lasagna, meat loaf, Kraft Dinner casseroles. Everything cooked from packages. Desserts on the last night, chocolate chip cookies, war cake, tomato soup cake, ginger snaps. The logic of it, desserts at the end, combined with the relentless irrationality of the feats of white-night cookery, made Sebastian feel reassured and uneasy at the same time, as unlikely as that sounds. To this day, memories of his mother taunt him with the same blend of queasy reassurance, the same dark knot of comforting discomfort he felt as each episode of his own personal freak show unfolded within known parameters: the mother-lump would stir at intervals and bake her heart out.

Nothing was that good or that bad. Everything was mixed. Yellow was yellowed, like a bone that had been buried, or teeth long hidden by stringent lips. A grimace might be a smile swimming through a sea of beige, or bone, or ivory, or eggshell. All the bland non-colours masked more than they displayed. None of these non-colours could be trusted, and that was another reason to tune out from colours altogether.

Grey never stood out in a black and white world. Grey was naturally the colour of dust and partially invisible. Grey was not a colour Sebastian noticed being released through the voice. There are no words which pronounce their inner grey souls as they are spoken. There is no display of grey, and that is how it sneaks up and attacks.

So much consistently overwhelmed Sebastian, at the time, that nothing could seem that weird. Everything was weird, so nothing was. During those turbulent years, with red so close, and grey hiding grey, who knew what anything really meant?

At about this time, Sebastian started private lessons with the blow-job teacher.

Part 5

FUTURE INSECTS

Now it was mostly like this. As if one
recent event had washed back everything
else and left her standing with her own
preoccupation. She could not help it. She
was ashamed. But she could not help.
There was only one purpose, ultimately one
person, in spite of the selfless aspiration,
which was hypocrisy, you were your own
focus, you were your own mind, your own
body.
– Patrick White, *The Living and the Dead*

Yes, the bitch, quietly, cruelly, she's pulling
me to pieces, bit by bit, slowly destroying
my whole being, second by second. And
now everything I do is full of death. Every
step brings her closer, every movement,
every breath, aids and abets her hateful
work. Breathing, sleeping, drinking, eating,
working, dreaming, everything we do
contains death. In fact living is dying!
– Guy de Maupassant, *Bel-Ami*

warning: may contain Scenes of Insecticide

Graphic scenes of violence against insects may overwhelm sensitive viewers.

The entire profitable pesticide industry devoted to these crimes against humanity.

Oh, of course, Sebastian knows that this is not literally a crime against humanity. Insects are not humanity. But aren't we all supposed to be connected? Shouldn't we, as humans, consistently try to demonstrate our best qualities?

How much humanity is shown if the motto is kill kill kill?

∞

Insecticide is genocide for insects.

∞

Can you imagine if genocide were a product advertised on television? Can you imagine if genocide were something you could buy at the store and keep under your sink in case you needed some? Wouldn't that concern you?

lard worms

Lard worms are actually tiny mites, distant relatives of spiders, and they live in your face. They make themselves at home, one species in hair follicles and another in the sebaceous glands. They dine on our fatty secretions, and under a microscope look like long tubular grubs with four pairs of stumpy little legs at one end.

We all have colonies of these things. Plugged-in head first and rarely come out. Around the nose and eyebrows. In the T-zone of grease.

Oh yes, and around the nipples. The starter colony.

The best thing about lard worms, perhaps, is that they are such selective and dainty consumers, sipping at liquids and rejecting even cell walls, that they produce no waste and require no excretory system.

This is certainly an enormous achievement for the lard worm.

This means they don't shit on your face.

Aren't you glad you have demodex follicle mites in your eyebrows and not cockroaches or mice?

Tom and Sebastian: what they have and what they do

1) They sleep together, mostly.

2) They listen to each other, to a degree.

3) They have a heart connection, and that feels special, but they also have crushes which don't mean anything. Technically, this is not an "open" relationship, because the crushes are in theory strictly hypothetical, and asymmetrical, and not going anywhere, therefore not "real."

4) Such as they are, Sebastian has crushes on straight men. These man-crushes seem to be self-limiting in nature.

5) Tom has flings with women (he certainly has in the past) or with "boys," the manly virgins he attracts with the bait of sensitivity. There is always a fresh crop of manly virgins. Tom loves his manly virgins.

6) Sebastian meanwhile is more or less doing the same thing: exploring an attraction; in his case, to sweet straight guys who are simultaneously chaste and

thoroughly experienced in the art of same-sex relations. Sebastian loves his manfriends.

fruitless obsessions

In the world of men, Sebastian often has man-crushes. But yes, otherwise, Sebastian is a gay entomologist.

Sebastian considers "gay entomologist" a ridiculous combination of words. Perhaps this is how Tom feels about "dyslexic bisexual." The two words are jammed together and rub against each other unpleasantly without achieving any additional meaning from the friction.

There is nothing gay about entomology. What is a gay entomologist? What does a gay entomologist think about?

Well, here is a glimpse inside the head of a gay entomologist in an odd moment. Sebastian's fantasy life is rich (stuff this good never actually happens):

Sebastian says to his man-crush: Let's lay on top of each other.

And he asks, Can we take off our shirts?

∞

Tom says a crush is a means to explore the completeness of the soul. But a crush on a straight man? What a waste of time.

Sebastian's soul will never be that complete.
Not in this bug's lifetime.

⌒⊃

"If I had a mantra," Sebastian stated, "that would be it:
No New Fruitless Obsessions."

Tom had laughed when Sebastian first expressed
the foundation for his new plan: to free himself, to
clear his head space; from now on, no new fruitless
obsessions. "Fruitless obsession does not specifically
mean a crush on a straight man," Sebastian said. "It
can mean anything. There are all kinds of fruitless
obsessions."

This was indeed Sebastian's earnest plan. Tom had
really laughed and said, "It's like a mantra."

Now Sebastian practices this routine, a throwaway
line to demonstrate his sense of humour. "If I *had* a
mantra, *had* a mantra; if I *had* a mantra, that would be
it. No New Fruitless Obsessions."

⌒⊃

Sebastian (it has been observed) can be gullible and
literal. Tom, in sport, tries to string him along.

Sebastian has become wary of Tom or anyone else
stringing him along. Being strung along has become
known as pulling a left-handed Buddhist.

Tom had obliquely (and innocently) mentioned left-
handed Buddhism, referring to the teachings of his sect,

which (in aspiration at least) incline towards bringing an element of choreography into the centreless dance of phenomena.

Sebastian had naturally accepted "left-handed Buddhist" to mean "left-handed people interested in Buddhism." Tom was left-handed. It was not that far-fetched to imagine a cohort of like-minded, left-handed Buddhists. There were gay Buddhists, after all, and Jewish Buddhists and Vietnamese Buddhists, so why not left-handed Buddhists? It was not so implausible.

Tom did not fully realize at the time how literal Sebastian could be, and so pushed the joke, embracing the absurdity. Unaccustomed to Tom's teasing nature, Sebastian was yet to be rendered completely suspicious and skeptical about everything Tom said.

To Tom, it was an obvious joke. Sebastian did not get obvious jokes in conflict with literal interpretations. When there was a literal interpretation, there was no obvious joke because the meaning was already totally implied. This was a revelation, a glimpse at what it might be like inside Sebastian's brain. A glimpse at how far literal went.

Sebastian did not, for example, glean any additional metaphoric implication, such as left-handed meaning sinister. Tom gave no hint that left-handed meant anything except being left-handed, and the fact that he pulled Sebastian's leg so far is how stringing someone along in a ridiculous story became known as pulling a left-handed Buddhist.

That "sinister" has been associated with aspects of

left-handedness is a connection that Tom has helped to make much more obvious with his teasing.

It became much harder to get anything past Sebastian. He had been trained, and was properly suspicious. Each of Tom's outrageous stories is automatically dismissed as being so much left-handed Buddhism, while displaying mild interest, to be polite, just in case. Tom rushes in with convincing details to prop up the narrative, and almost always turns out to be one of Tom's simply outrageous stories, one of the many incredible things that just happen to Tom, not left-handed Buddhism after all. When things are almost always turning out a certain way, this is how a person gets lulled into complacency and forgets to question what he is being told. This is the danger of belief.

Sebastian could easily spend much more time worrying about the difference between things that really happened and things that Tom has probably just made up, but as we have all heard by now, Sebastian's new mantra is: no new fruitless obsessions.

Pulling a left-handed Buddhist is also something that can be done to Tom.

He can be pulled, and yanked, and tugged.

more lard worms

Sebastian knows he is host to many.

Sebastian has never met his lard worms but knows they are there. Unlike many other entomologists, he has never tried to scrape ectoparasites off his own face to eyeball under a microscope.

Sebastian could not imagine, for a moment's bleak amusement, wrenching those little demodex from their cozy lairs, just to peer at their dismembered carcasses. He would not dare to eye the carnage.

Still, Sebastian is sure they are there, living near his nose and eyebrows, in the greasy T-zone of intimacy. The nuzzle zone. The mother colony around the nipples.

He is sure that his lard worms and Tom's lard worms have met.

Which came first? Sebastian wonders. Nuzzling, or lard worms?

Perhaps lard worms themselves, he speculates, created the nuzzling behaviour in their hosts. Lard worms developed nuzzling as a means of meeting other lard worms living in distant colonies. Buried head first in the forehead, the mite's stumpy little limbs manipulated the levers of power in the lurching meat puppets, orchestrating the nuzzling impulse in their clumsy hosts.

These insects live in your eyebrows and crawl out at night and mate on your forehead!

Sebastian doubts that this statement is strictly true. He despised the sensationalism of so much reporting from the world of insects. Has any such nighttime forehead mating ever actually been observed?

He thinks not.

Many insects, you see, can choose to mate or not. If no mate is handy, a plucky little fellow will just go ahead and reproduce all on its own. It is customary to refer to such enterprising individuals as female, although Sebastian, as a scientist, feels that those possessed of such cloning technology are beyond gender assignment. Gender assignment, a binary impulse, is irrelevant when one can clone. To be able to clone oneself is to be like an angel, to be outside or beyond gender.

The lard worm has this cloning technology and do-it-yourself spirit. When the lard worm arrives in new territory and is all alone, she plunks herself down headfirst into a pore and gives virgin birth to clones in a process called parthenogenesis.

She then mates with her sons.

Now, she is clearly female.

Sebastian has tiny little follicle mites on his mind, and

on his face. He has never met them, but he knows they are there.

Lard worms are extremely common and yet are little studied. They normally cause no problems in humans. There is no way to get rid of them, and they may even be of benefit in maintaining pores and ducts, functioning as a type of biological nanotechnology for sweaty-faced primates.

Lard worms are part of us, and they live on our face. And around our nipples.

But they don't shit there.

A lard worm's first words? Please, no fiber!

Nonsense, says Sebastian. The words of a lard worm? But the sentiment is true. The lard worm feeds on liquids, rejecting even cell walls. Keeps the oily secretions free-flowing on our face, maintaining the ductwork in exchange for a sip of grease.

Thank you, tireless demodex, unsung insect hero.

the natural solution

For all his spiritual development, much of Tom still operates as a hunter and gatherer.

Tom is a searcher.

Hunting and gathering for things to bring home.

Tom brought home scabies.

Scabies, like lard worms, are also tiny little mites who make themselves at home in our skin. However, these mites are another story.

These mites are a problem, because they are insanely itchy and especially fond of the baby-tender skin between the fingers, on the neck, or on the penis.

Tom was infested near both hips, in front. You could actually see little trails burrowed through his skin along the crease where torso met legs. Some were scratches and some were burrows. Mites, at home in your skin: nothing could be creepier. Not living in a duct or pore and minding its own business like a lard worm, but actually tunnelling right through the skin like prairie dogs heading into a cold winter.

There is nothing cute and user-friendly about

scabies. Scabies are the gift that keeps on itching. Just the memory of scabies is enough to make you half-scratch to death. Sebastian is quite able to draw the line when necessary, thank you, and he drew it at scabies.

Tom also brought home food, laughter, books, crystals and other rocks,[17] clothes, and boys.

Sebastian pretends not to notice the boys, whose presence lingers in ephemeral traces, mostly wispy odours.

Sebastian does notice the creative vegan cuisine, the laughter, the volcanic glass, the red shirt he would never have bought for himself, but does not mention the skunky boy who showered in their apartment earlier that afternoon, put his clothes back on, and became fresh skunky boy.

Sebastian could smell him, could almost see him in a way. There was a wild tang in wispy traces, and Sebastian sensed a tall, blurry manboy slouched on the couch with his legs spread as far as baggy jeans would allow. The wild ones, their jeans always half on half off, never reappeared once they made their escape.

Sebastian said not a word about the tangy wisps, or the blue excitement spilling from Tom's voice.

---

[17] Actual geological products such as rose quartz, obsidian, and hematite. Tom does not use drugs of any nature (unless religion can truly be considered an opiate).

They laughed at some stupid joke, purple bouncing around them like a cocoon.

It's not that Tom had secrets. What he had was privacy.

Scabies helped bring them closer. Shared possessions require negotiation.

Sebastian was possessed by an itch at the underbelly of his triceps. He noticed a branching line up the inside of his elbow.

Tom was delegated to go to a clinic, and the doctor recommended the cure-all killer shampoo, applied head to toe, co-ordinated with the treatment of Sebastian (and any other intimates, who all must be informed). Habitat control was vital. All bedding, clothes, towels, washed in hot water. Dried in the dryer.

The cure-all killer shampoo, as we all know, carried the risk of permanent nerve damage.

Sebastian wanted to try a "natural" alternative.

"This is irony, isn't it?" he asked Tom. "You, the hippie, want to rush out and buy the quick toxic solution promoted by commercial science, and me, the commercial scientist, want to search out the natural solution which is in harmony with all things. Except, of course, for the scabies themselves, which must be discouraged with extreme prejudice. If relocation proves impractical."

"What?" Tom asked.

"That was a joke."

Sebastian was quite pleased with himself.

"I just want to get rid of them," Tom said. "Now that I know they are there. Tunnelling through my skin. Through me. I am just so itchy I can't stand it."

"It is ironic isn't it? This is karma, yes? Somehow? You want to use pesticides directly on *me*. A neurotoxin. After what already happened."

There are times when all goes silent and this means a topic has gone as far as it ever is going to go. It is not good to talk beyond this point. When you reach that point the only thing to do is to wait and see what Tom is thinking.

Tom cleared his throat.

"What natural solution?" he asked.

The natural solution, like the final solution, was a euphemism for the same conclusion: extermination.

Olive oil is where they started with the natural solutions. Oil offers a mechanical approach to killing small insects such as mites by smothering them. The surface tension of the oil slick blocks their breathing. Basically, they drown.

The mites persisted. They dug in and kept getting greeted with something new. Every itch was monitored and examined under a magnifying glass. Tom and Sebastian would consult on the prognosis. They called this nit-picking, although it wasn't.

They graduated to olive oil flavoured with oil of oregano. They tried olive oil mixed with other essential oils, peppermint, rosemary, and extract of neem (known in India as the toothbrush tree because people break off twigs and use them to brush their teeth).

They explored the world through their natural solutions, which were messy, but since they had to wash the bedding all the time anyway, they didn't care.

Eventually, the natural solution did work. They were using olive oil mixed with Australian tea tree oil, so that was seen as being the most effective, if not the final, solution.

The branching burrow had been the first sketchy draft of a suburb, but the development failed. Never took off. It could have been the tea tree oil, but maybe the upstarts had already been exhausted by the neem or the oregano and finally just all drowned one day in a wave of olive oil.

Skin became so silky. Oil massages easily slid into other bonding activities. Every inch was manhandled and slick.

Tom and Sebastian managed to survive scabies, even as they did their best to exterminate the local colonies.

Tom liked the tea tree oil. He liked the smell. It smelled sharply clean without being too harsh. He trusted the harshness. When he imagined feeling the tingle of a scabies mite stirring in his skin, Tom would rub a drop of tea tree oil right on the tingly spot. Tom called this "asking for oil," the mite was asking for oil, and he rubbed it in.

In this way, a natural solution and the final solution converged.

Tom's mindfulness practice became being aware of an itch, but not being attached to an itch. An itch is just a sensation. And sensation is just the mind. See the mind, see how it works, and let it go.

And if the itch doesn't go away when you let it go, it's probably a scabies mite.

Asking for oil.

what Tom smells like

The armpit is always there, even if you can't always see it.

As elusive as a forest beast, it can appear at any moment, and disappear in a flash.

Tom's armpits always make themselves known, even when they can't be seen.

When shirtless and cuddling together, or debriefing, the armpit on the far side of the chest bristles with a jaunty pit-hawk, the crest of hair displayed when the arm is down, the darkness announcing the cream. The hedge of hair is a backdrop for the line of the chest, jutting up jagged like green plastic sushi garnish, sticking out, framing the horizon of the chest. The pit-hawk, at just the right angle, sets off a squarish-profiled nipple surrounded by a corona of long coarse black hairs. Tom likes to hold these hairs straight out from his nipple and say, "Look. Look closely, see there that circle? It's Hairhenge."

And that was just the far armpit.

The near armpit gets even better.

The near armpit is fabulous to look at. An armpit was the thing which enabled Sebastian to believe he understood the motivation of landscape gardeners.

Each of Tom's armpits was a thing of beauty, offering a brush with nature melded with architectural nuance and structural integrity. One could look but not always touch, could not gently trace the contours at the intersection of life and limb. Tom was too ticklish for fingers running through the underbrush and foothills. He didn't like it.

If tickled, Tom would clamp his arms down, both pit-hawks bristling like single furry quotes bracketing the torso.

Sebastian had to promise. Promise not to touch, unless he was touching in certain ways that Tom liked. He could kiss his armpit, for example. His chest or his armpit. Tom loved that. Tom loved men to touch and tug at Hairhenge. Tom loved a nice armpit kiss. But Sebastian did not do that often. At such close range, no matter how sweeping his infatuation, and even though Tom no longer wears deodorant and smells only of himself, the smell could be too much for Sebastian.

Mostly, he liked looking at armpits.

Tom is generous with the twins.

The twins are very similar, yet unique.

Tom's armpits are sweet-bellied displays offering warmth and the silkiest skin. They smell of the planet.

Each briny cove offering a split island of underbrush. Whimsical tufts, moist at their base, curl into darkening tendrils as inviting as mammals. Web-footed sea otters came to mind. Playful and inquisitive and often upside down. Begging to be explored, Tom's armpit was a nest of kelp fronds parting to the currents. A wispiness anchored to a body.

Winking its own code, each of Tom's armpits signals the tides of renewal and withdrawal. Of openness and closure. Of invitation and protection. The compression and release of desire.

pet projects

The research that Sebastian had most set his heart on devoting his life to was the study of polyctenids, the specialized parasites of bats. These are true bugs, and often called bat bugs, although that appellation sounds inelegant.

Sebastian thought these creatures were the coolest things. Bugs who lived on bats. Blind and wingless, bat bugs are highly modified ectoparasites, and closely related to bed bugs. Bed bugs were probably bat bugs who made the switch to humans in a cave long ago. A switch to humans who returned night after night to the same dwelling. And then, eventually, in a total lifestyle reinvention, moved with people and their belongings all over the world.

Now bed bugs are universal in the human population and widely studied, while bat bugs remain somewhat unknown (except through inference).

These external parasites live on the blood of their hosts.

These tiny, blind, wingless bloodsuckers specialize on one particular hard-to-groom part of the body, the ear for example, of one kind of bat, who might live (let's say) in a cave on an island. That is what Sebastian wanted to devote his life to, a foray into the unknown frontiers of science, but there is no money in insects on bats in a cave on an island.

The mysteries of the polyctenids, living on birds and bats, remain intact.[18]

With so little known about the blind ectoparasites of bats, there was room to make a real contribution to science. There would be much for Sebastian to discover. Even where bats roost is largely unknown. It is unknown how many species of bats support distinctly specialized colonies of parasites. This is one of the many fields in entomology wide open for pure research; and where are the resources spent? In the killing fields.

This whole family of bloodsuckers has bizarre habits. Mating occurs with a traumatic insemination which involves rupturing an opening into the female where there was none before and depositing a sperm mass. The young develop inside the female's abdomen and are born live.

In many families who practice traumatic insemination, homosexual rape is quite common. Freed from a need for strict engagement with specific female

---

[18] Tom was fascinated by one type of bird parasite, a flightless fly, found on owls in North America. Owls, eagles, and condors. He found something strangely beautiful about the idea of a wingless fly tagging along for the ride and soaring over the mountains, forests, plains, and coast.

sexual structures, males in these families are a bit unfocussed and will attempt to drill into other males, nymphs, non-receptive females, insects from other species, and even inanimate objects roughly the right shape, size, or smell.

Perhaps, if one is blind and flightless and secluded in a bat's pungent roost, one doesn't get out much. Under these conditions, a bat bug may attempt to hump whatever is within reach.

There are bat bugs out there with Sebastian's name on them. Or there so easily could be, he is sure, if only he could mount the expedition to that cave on that island and study the ectoparasites of bats living in what must be very foul and stinky tropical caves.

There are bugs in those caves dining on blood from a bat's ear just waiting for Sebastian to come along and give them his name.

Waiting to be discovered by science.

Hopefully, before being wiped off the face of the earth.

doing it right

Sebastian finds it easy to love straight men. His manfriends.
   Sebastian loves what is.
   He loves everything just the way it is.
   He loves people for what they are. If someone is a nice straight man, that is very easy to love.

Sebastian does not understand Tom's assertion that Sebastian loves subterranean men. That Sebastian wastes his time digging for these buried men, and then eventually exclaiming in frustration, "Hey, you are so buried! Are you dead? Buried alive? Or just straight?"
   According to Tom, that is Sebastian's recurring epiphany. His moment of awakening. When he sees a subterranean man as deep and buried.

Sebastian finds it natural to love men no matter how subterranean. He does not question it. It is so easy. They are very undemanding. Their expectations are easily exceeded. They are never critical of truncated emotional displays.

Sebastian does not see what is supposedly so pointless about a man-crush. What is the point anyway of any crush?

Besides, love is not always a choice.

If that is what love is, a crush. Whatever it should be called, Sebastian loves straight men. He loves his man-crushes and his manfriends. This love manifests as inordinate fondness for nice straight men who also (usually) happen to be especially cute.

Sebastian follows simple guidelines in the pursuit of man-crushes and manfriends. One loves what is, that is important. And if what you are loving is a straight man, never develop any sort of romantic or reciprocal expectation. The entire process of dealing with straight men is a great exercise in not having any attachment to outcome.

At the same time, as much as possible under the circumstances, expect to be surprised.

People use the word love but do not love, Sebastian has observed. What they call love is merely a vehicle to express need. They say, "I love you," but they mean, "I want you to take care of my needs." When you love someone and do not expect anything back in return, that is love.

Loving a manfriend and expecting nothing in return, that is love.

To love a straight man teaches patience.

Sebastian has patience. And no expectations. But still, is surprised.

hugging from behind

Sebastian really likes to hug from behind. He likes the solid feel of it, the back to his front, and he likes having the access to the sides and front of the torso, with his arms and hands. He likes the solid warm contact pressed against his chest and belly, and he likes the way a bum can nestle into his lap.

Hugging from behind is a special way to touch the bum.

Sebastian also likes the view. The back of an ear, jutting out like sculpture. One perpendicular end of the semicircular jawbone. The line of a cheekbone like a blunt horizon framing: what can be handled and what is beyond. The slivers of face, oblique and manageable.

Murmurs like green soup simmering around them.

Warmth settles between.

Backs are irresistible, Sebastian finds.

∞

Hugging from behind works its own magic in its own way. Body language is spoken and understood. Disputes are raised, negotiated, and cuddled into irrelevance.

Hugging from behind is both sexual and non-sexual.

(Sebastian is becoming much more able to accommodate paradox.)

It is sexual because the ass is right there, resting on the cock, and often there are erections, pressed into buttocks. Hugging from behind is sexual because it leads to sex.

Hugging from behind is non-sexual because there are other elements too, besides genitals and sex. There is chesting. Chesting is an activity where two men bring their chests together. There are many pretenses developed to mask and blur the pursuit of same-sex chesting, such as wrestling and horseplay, and plain old-fashioned hugging.

Hugging from behind is a form of chesting, involving one chest and one back of chest.

Hugging from behind, although both sexual and non-sexual, is widely perceived as extremely intimate and suitable only for lovers, usually in private, although also acceptable for lovers at crowded public events, like watching a parade or concert in the park where everyone is standing. In public, hugging from behind is a possession-display.

A straight man, hugged from behind, is likely to feel extremely uncomfortable. He will not relax into it. He does not want his bum touched in any special way.

Hugging from behind is something Tom and Sebastian do a lot, and it is both sexual and non-sexual, like everything else they do.

They do this in private, so it is not a possession-display. They curl up together, back-to-front chesting, or spooning, and sometimes they talk.

These pillow talks are quiet and low-key, but cover more territory more quickly than vertical and animated free-ranging discussions.

Hugging from behind serves many functions, and it is one of Sebastian's most favourite things.

means not // slogans

Awareness means not being afraid of losing focus.

∽

Awareness means having a focus, but not being too
concerned about keeping that focus.

∽

Means not forgetting the slogans. Means not being
obsessed with them either. They're there when you need
them. They're always there.

A slogan is like a mantra, except a slogan
makes more sense. A mantra is mostly like singing,
and abstract. A slogan has words in a language you
understand.

Tom uses slogans every day. His slogans vary,
but most are part of a teaching called *lojong*, used by
Tibetan monks since before there was Tibet. Tibetan
Buddhists are obviously thoroughly familiar with
the experience of unrelenting angst in their lives.
Generations of monks have relied on *lojong* slogans to
help cope with the tortures of mind.

Tom says they help. A couple of his favorite slogans are, "Drive all blame into one," and, "All dharma is a dream."

Tom is very attached to ancient Tibetan slogans, and noticeably less impressed by the slogans made up by Sebastian yesterday.

"No new fruitless obsessions," for example, was not embraced despite its obvious wisdom.

Another slogan, "Everything is on the path," has achieved partial recognition and sparked some debate. Total acceptance is pending, following a review concerning the location of the path in relation to where we currently might be.

The Tibetan line was, "Bring whatever occurs to the path."

"Whatever occurs, is in the path," Sebastian argued. "Where else would it be? Everything is in the path."

"Bring whatever occurs to the path," Tom said.

"Everything," Sebastian insisted, "is on the path. Or in the path."

"Whatever occurs," Tom said.

"Everything," Sebastian agreed.

"Yes."

"Time is all a dream, anyway," Sebastian said. "I don't see why you are so concerned about the little words in a big dream."

"I am not concerned," Tom said. "All dharma is a dream."

"Good," Sebastian said.

bagpiping

The way Tom smelled, whatever it was, Sebastian wanted more. That is what can be said, at its simplest: Tom smelled like more. Sebastian wanted to keep smelling that smell. Smelling Tom gave Sebastian something to do during lengthy debriefings, during chesting and pillow talks. Tom can talk a lot, has much to say, and smelling Tom gave Sebastian something to do because he does not always listen. But he always smells Tom's smell. He breathes it in, a green and blue bottom note, and lets it swim among the teal and purple paisley of Tom's story.

What Tom smells like is something out of this world. And yet he smells like everything in the world.

If Tom has been eating hard-boiled eggs, his gas in the night can smell like sulphur. The rotten-egg sulphur smell. This is what hell is supposed to smell like. For good reason.

Armpits are more than a feast for the eyes. Armpits are also for lovemaking.

Intercourse with an armpit is called axillary

intercourse, except no one ever calls it that. What people call armpit fucking, if they mention it at all, is a pit-job, or now bagpiping.

At its simplest, bagpiping involves one penis and one armpit.

Bagpiping, as the new term, originated at Scotchtoberfest.

Scotchtoberfest is like Oktoberfest and involves lots of drinking, but takes place in Scotland, not Germany. Drinking may explain the armpit as destination, not as a personal choice, but as more or less a happy accident (or at least, one happily not clearly recalled). Small-minded types, unable to think outside the box, presume that bagpiping is a kind of botched thing, the result of drink and bumbling, and not something that arose from a clear firm desire for the particular treats of a squishy moist pit-job.

In any event, bagpiping happens.

And not just in Scotland.

Coming soon, in an armpit near you.

A confession Sebastian has yet to make out loud:
    "I'm into armpits."

A sentence which perplexed and transfixed Sebastian when he read it in a flippant sexual advice column:

"Foot-job is the new bagpiping."

But, he had to protest, they are nowhere near the same thing. Foot-job is *not* the new bagpiping.

success stories

Tom takes on beautiful troubled youths as a kind of project.

There are success stories: an organic produce boy, now a shiatsu therapist; a street kid who graduated from "spanging" to subsidized housing and programming at a gay lesbian bisexual and transgendered film festival.

There are also names and people he cannot remember.

They are all part of who he is, even if he cannot remember them specifically. "They all made me," Tom claims. "They made me who I am. They made me as I am. I am their success story, as much as they are mine."

Tom plays with their spirituality, these boys. He seduces them by giving them a taste of their own power. He helps to connect them to themselves, and this is enough of an unexpected flirtation with power that Tom reaps the benefits, and is involved in the transaction and in the encounter.

What?

"Men are driven by sex," Tom says. "And most just

drive straight past me. Although a few have stopped for the night, before going on with their journey."

Tom has the key somehow to unlock these manboys. He inserts his special key, wiggles it around a bit, and the boy learns a thing or two. Soon afterward, in the blink of an eye, the boy becomes a man. His own man.

Tom does not date the kind of gay boys who are determined, silly, aggressive bottoms, overfed and undernourished, maturing into fruition as streaked, puffy, too-tanned, frantic clichés of the sort one is not allowed to mention, it's so embarrassing and so true.

The type Tom goes for is sensitive and in transition (in the classical sense, meaning a lifestyle and/or self-concept metamorphosis, but not a gender reassignment). What attracts Tom beyond all reason is a manboy exploring the boundaries of a gentle, proud, fierce, but uncertain masculinity. Young and naïve enough to believe in his essential spiritual nature.

Possibly bi-curious, and that is where Tom slips in.

Tom is bi, and the manboy, curious.

Nothing could be more natural.

It is only natural too that each one of these volatile, transitioning manboys does not last long. They almost always swear to keep in touch, and swear to do so passionately, because everything is done passionately.

Sometimes they even do keep in touch for a short time.

The success stories, however, make everything worthwhile.

The reason Tom is vulnerable to manboys is because he is lost in his memory of himself at that age. When he took over his own life. At that age was the first time Tom fell in love with himself and what he might do. He so impressed himself, by leaving the Farm and going to the city, and more than surviving – totally reinventing everything. While nuturing and confirming who he was and staying true to his nature.

Who could not fall in love with that?

Tom's ego lapped it up.

At the same time, in a modest displacement, Tom fell in love with human potential. Tom fell in love with the amazing human ability to do something brave and foolish and risky, like leave, like strike out on one's own, like fall in love, like make out with a dead-sexy stranger. To take a moment, and fall right into the heart of it.

All this risk-management is easier for the young. Tom did things when he was twenty he only dreams about now. He was so brave, and so foolish, and so successful at being brave and foolish without really caring.

There is this phase, the angry manboy phase, where one does not care about anything, because one has been so proud and wounded and kicked around and taken for granted. One is too angry to feel. And yet at the same time one feels so deeply.

The power generated by those poles of disparity is enormous. One feels a great numbness.

What Tom is in love with to this day is himself at that age, when feelings ran so powerfully deep and hidden. He felt free, because he could just leave. And he did leave. He left angry manboy at the Farm and he walked away.

He was strong enough to do what had to be done. Tom may appear easy-going, but that display shows a desire to be in control. And sometimes the only control was to leave. Tom had the power to leave. He'd exercised it before. It had transformed his life. That is how he became easy-going.

When Tom sees these manboys stuck in the heart of their own displacement, he cannot help but respond, because he feels he has something to teach.

Out of strength, he has left. Not just out of fear or a need to escape. Tom has used strength to leave, and to arrive at a better place. He has done it, so he thinks it is the best thing to be done. And he thinks he can help the manboys leave displacement behind and move into their own power.

Tom can help these manboys, and he does help them, although perhaps not all of them realize it at the time. Not every manboy makes or receives a deep impression. Of course, each one is very special in his own way, but after a while even special is not enough to make you memorable.

Tom says, impermanence. Whenever the topic veers off to forgotten manboys, Tom says, impermanence. Impermanence is the consolation prize whenever a better response is temporarily out of reach.

When one talks about the success stories, impermanence means they are off doing other things now. They have "gone on."

What Sebastian wants to know is this: How long does interest have to be maintained to successfully compound into a success story?

In situations like these, interest rates have been observed to be highly variable.

making Tom // the one

Tom has pointed out that if there is just one person, Sebastian talks. But if there is more than one person, Sebastian does not talk. He goes silent. He listens but he does not talk.

So Tom said that it was best if he was that one person. What he meant was, when Tom and Sebastian see each other they should just see each other. That is what they try to do. They are alone, together.

This makes their time together kind of concentrated and isolated, like an egg or an embryo, which although alive was self-contained all in the one place at once.

Of course both of them, Tom especially, had lives outside the life they had together. They had a nest together but both of them, especially Tom, made forays out into the world and maybe talked about it, maybe not. There was always pillow talk, but everything was not always talked about.

There is much not to dwell on here, such as the paradox of being "alone together," plus all the things that are best not to mention, because even asking can sometimes be too much. Men do not like questions, but Sebastian always has lots of questions; although it is true he does not like being asked. He does not like to think about what cannot be answered or cannot be asked, and these thoughts about nothing are the ones that get stuck inside Sebastian's head and can never find their way out again.

∞

Some questions make Tom laugh.

∞

Sebastian makes Tom laugh.

There are different ways to make Tom laugh.

There are the foolproof ways which work every time, and there are ways which are not foolproof and may or may not work.

One foolproof way to make Tom laugh is to hug him while he is talking, squeeze gently but sporadically, and maintain quizzical eye contact while pretending to listen. The eye contact penetrates Tom. Laughter then becomes a force from within which takes over. Even Tom sometimes cannot look and keep talking. Sebastian can feel it growing in his arms, the helpless laughter asserting itself, gathering strength and making itself known.

Shards of laughter breaking into the voice.

If he stares into the face of it, he can summon it, and see it before it arrives. There is so much power with the eyes, now that Sebastian has learned to use it.

Sebastian feels these are secrets, these programming overrides, which allow one to make someone do something.

Like making someone laugh. Or cry.

A good chesting, Sebastian knows, and Tom becomes a different person.

There are many ways of making Tom laugh, but Sebastian does not wish, at this time, to provide any more detailed instructions.

Part 6

THE MANY-LEGGED

Men are just bigger, more complicated
gall wasps.
– Alfred C. Kinsey

For Kinsey, then, labels such as
"homosexual" and "heterosexual" did not
make sense. People engaged in homosexual
acts; they were not homosexuals.
Therefore, the only proper use for the word
"homosexual" was as an adjective, not as
a noun. Pressing this point vigorously,
he declared, "It would encourage clearer
thinking on these matters if persons
were not characterized as heterosexual
or homosexual, but as individuals who
have had certain amounts of heterosexual
experience and certain amounts of
homosexual experience."
– James H. Jones, *Alfred C. Kinsey:*
A Public/Private Life

was green on

Sebastian was not sure how much of what Tom says was strictly true.

But then, Sebastian was not sure how much of anything is really true. If things are just a dream, as the Buddhists claim, nothing was really true because it was all a dream. And a dream is just a dream and dreams have no concern for truth. That is how a dream can be a dream.

Having an affair was like a dream. Having an affair was all about keeping the truth offstage. Having an affair was like a dream about a secret.

And keeping the secret. Without the secret, an affair might not be so interesting.

Sebastian could smell her before he met her, or even knew her name or heard a word about her. Being fanciful and retrospective, Sebastian would describe the smell as civet cat chained to a juniper bush. A musky martini: vaporous, with accents of lemongrass and a strong backbeat of oregano. Or catnip.

There was a greenness too about Tom that

Sebastian noticed but did not comment on. When Tom was green on someone, he was suffused. Shoots of fresh spring green stood out like a sudden row of trees against an April sky. Deep forest green percolated as deep as innermost feelings. Dark, bright, everything, green.

His lips parted, his expression vague and hopeful, Tom was green all over.

Sebastian could smell her. It had to be a her. Only with women did Tom keep a crush so secret. If it was a guy Tom was all green over and crushing out on, he would have already told Sebastian everything (while admitting nothing). Would have already been talking about this wonderful amazing guy, who was so friendly and wonderful and amazing in so many special ways. Without ever admitting he had a crush. In fact, would deny it if asked point blank. Act startled even. What? No! Not my type. Too – [pause for ambiguous dismissive] Too – *smooth*. Too – *trendy*. *Over-groomed*.

When Tom was green on someone, his voice gave him away.

Too – *emphatic*.

Too – *green*.

Sebastian recognized green. Sebastian had a certain familiarity with green in all its greenness. When he first met Tom, and Tom repeated the words, "The future is insects," or whatever was said in the shade of an oak tree at the edge of the reception, Sebastian saw and felt a sprawling green, in the same moment everywhere all around and overhead, a deep green like a shower of algae. The green burst forth from the seeds of Tom's words. In that moment Sebastian flashed, green is for go, and he was right. He flashed and he was right. That was meeting Tom.

Sebastian knew green.

Now when Sebastian saw threads of green in Tom's voice, the emotional display was not for him.

The green was not the same green.

Green still meant go, but not his go.

When Tom was green on someone, Sebastian ignored him. He did not interrogate Tom, nor attempt to seduce or distract him away from it.

There was no competing anyway. When Tom was green on someone, he swanned around in his own fantasy and was blind to everything but his vision. The vision was lush and verdant and nothing else compared. Ribbons of green wrapped each of Tom's words as he spoke, oblivious to the present. A dreamy background green hovered around him even when Tom fell silent, and Sebastian seriously wondered how much information slid around in life, from one category to another, from seeing and hearing and knowing and feeling, as if labels and separations and distinctions didn't really matter.

Sebastian wondered if everything he had learned so far really added up to much he could count on, if he really had to, for example, in a time of potential crisis.

There have been developments.

Sebastian does not need Tom's voice to see the colours for how Tom is feeling. Sebastian can see colours with Tom all the time if he wants to, not just when Tom speaks his packaged words, decorated with the tattered garlands of feelings, and rainbows of hope and longing.

Sebastian sees colours everywhere now, especially around Tom. Colours sparked by just his thoughts, but still, most remarkably, by thoughts of Tom. Distracted by his secret crush, a fresh green bursting gleefulness, rolling in catnip with mouth wide open, fangs displayed to the silent observer.

Tom was very green, all over again.

the brutal truth

Sebastian cherished a flippant advice column called "Brute Love." The topics covered were never remotely relevant to Sebastian (the best dildo for a virgin; the etiquette of hooking up with the roommate's mother), but the advice was meant to be modern, and aspired to brutal frankness saturated with sarcasm. This alleged candor was the best part. Sebastian was intrigued to glimpse what people might say to each other if they could speak freely and get away with it. Mostly, people talk through opaque filters and thus it is impossible to know what they are thinking or feeling, because they never say. And never give themselves away. They never show a thing.

Sebastian swore by "Brute Love" as a breath of fresh air.

He found reassurance in these intimate portraits. Again and again, in comparison, Sebastian turned out to be definitely not the biggest bonehead on the planet. The message to be extracted was: the more obvious the problem, the more likely some hapless idiot will require advice in order to see the brutal truth.

Everyone has their own special blind spots.

Reading the column on this one particular day,

Sebastian's heart did a peculiar little flip-stop in his chest. Yes, a flip-stop. It did this twisty little flip, and then stopped, a dead stop, his ears roaring, until Sebastian wrenched his eyes away from the free alternative weekly.

He gazed off into space, looking at nothing, his lips rounded into a silent "oh." Sebastian was panicked and searching for that great forgiving space where he could just bliss out into ignorance. An ignorance grander than any incoming information.

The great forgiving space where there was room for everything to be ignored or forgotten: that was where Sebastian suddenly wanted to go.

But it was not as easy for Sebastian to escape into the blur as it used to be. He could, but he couldn't. Not really. Not like he used to. Sebastian wondered, was he more present? Or less scared? More aware? Whatever it was, he could not simply let himself slide away from whatever was in front of him and pretend he did not see it, did not care.

There was to be no more pretending.

Even when he really wanted to avoid something confusing and riddled with horror. It was hard even to look at Tom right now.

He was not sure what he was looking at.

The topic in this week's "Brute Love" which had so alarmed Sebastian concerned a man with a bisexual boyfriend.

The bisexual boyfriend had a girlfriend.

The girlfriend was pregnant.

The bisexual boyfriend broke up with his gay boyfriend and now was living with the pregnant girlfriend.

The question was, the man still wanted to "help" his bisexual ex-boyfriend (ex-bisexual boyfriend?) and wondered how. He believed the struggling young couple needed him, financially and emotionally. Even though clearly dumped, he "sensed mixed messages" about his continuing role in the relationship, and wondered how to proceed.

The letter-writer signed himself, "No Longer Sure I Even Want to Babysit."

This letter left Sebastian feeling congested, mentally. His head was swelling with an inside-out purple darkness like an eggplant sprouting from his lizard brain.[19] His eyes glazed out and he could read no further. He did not need to know the rest. There was no need to read more. He put off reading the dreaded brutal truth as long as he could.

As long as he could turned out to be about ninety minutes.

The advice columnist was predictably sarcastic and quite frankly judgmental concerning Babysitter's perceived lack of spine, balls, and personal insight.

In summary, the Brute advised that bisexual men were called bisexual because after being with another man for a while, eventually the odds mount to the point where if the right woman trolls past, or even any

---

[19] An eggplant itself, not an eggplant plant.

woman, the bisexual man goes, "Bye!"[20]

Apparently (if one can believe an advice columnist in a free alternative weekly), the word was originally spelled "bye-sexual" or even "buy-sexual" but became corrupted.

None of this was information Sebastian cared to absorb.

Now he was going to fester.

This was not Sebastian's letter to the advice columnist. Let's be clear about that. But Sebastian did have a bisexual boyfriend. And that bisexual boyfriend did have a girlfriend –

This is where (it must be admitted) Sebastian has not been very successful in not thinking about a particular topic and related uncertainties.

Tom has a girlfriend.

Probably.

Maybe.

He *probably* has a girlfriend, but still. That was enough to make Sebastian realize he should get used to the idea.

Whatever the idea was.

What was the idea?

Was the idea that Tom's girlfriend would make Tom revert to his original "bye-sexuality"?

Was Tom going to go "bye" for good?

---

[20] Otherwise, it means he has turned gay.

Sebastian knows these questions are unanswerable. The lack of good answers has never put a stop to questions.

There are even questions that might be best left unanswered.

There was so much for Sebastian to think about here, and to not think about, that at any point in time it was impossible to not be thinking about something.

Tom says nothing has changed, but what can he possibly mean when he says that?

Everything always changes.

And everyone always pretends that everything will always be the same. When it never is. Things are never the same, so what is Tom talking about?

Mr. Impermanence is now, all of a sudden, claiming nothing has changed.

Sebastian did not know what to believe.

the story of

The story of the girlfriend is the story of Tom's new career as a pet therapist.

The story of Tom's new career as a pet therapist (or animal intuitive, or pet psychic, or animal interpreter) is the story of other careers never really taking off.

The story of a career in spiritual marketing never taking off hopefully is never traced back to a lack of support in "flaky things" emanating from a significant other in Tom's life.

Sebastian had vigorously pooh-poohed the merchandise machine fueling Tom's spiritual pursuits. Instead of career sabotage, this almost prescient pooh-poohing may be viewed as career enabling, since the need for a career change enabled Tom to move into his chosen field of inter-species communication, a big step towards fulfilling his soul quest to facilitate deeper, more meaningful relationships between people and non-human companions.

People and non-human companions, in real terms, turns out to be women and cats.

Women with cats and money.

Such women, with their major cat problems, tend not to have boyfriends nearby and this, unfortunately, is where Tom seems to come in.

The story of Tom's new profession is also the story of an undoubtedly neurotic cat, and how this neurotic feline, a Siamese, lured Tom into its orbit, possibly for no more reason than its own droll amusement and a back rub.

Cats move into your aura, Tom claims. This particular Siamese cat was the reason a certain youngish woman contacted Catalyst and invited Tom into her sprawling ground-level west-side garden suite, asking, "What on earth do you suppose has gotten into Katakana? She hasn't been the same since the move."

Mostly, Tom talks to disposable-incomed folks about their pets. It's a companion service to having a companion animal. People pay people to listen to them talk about their pets.

People talk about their pets, but really, they always talk about themselves.

And Tom listens.

Catalyst Counselling: free in-home assessment, guaranteed breakthrough results.

People (so far, only women) pay Tom for his apparent ability to facilitate the inter-species relationship they are having with their own companion animal. Tom reads the situation, observing closely, and provides intuitive feedback which he makes up on the spot. Results are goal-oriented, such as convincing some evil vixen of a cat not to shit on the bed. No shitting on the bed is a very common goal in these matters. And one easy to measure.

Oddly, something here seemed to work. Goals were met. Evil vixens were diverted and placated and reassured. Duvets saved. And this is how Tom met a certain young woman who has so far remained nameless.

Her name is Clara.

Clara was having trouble with her cat, who seemed anxious. Restless. Clara became possessed with the idea that Tom ("Catalyst") would be able to fix this situation. Katakana was wound up, howling sometimes like you would not believe. Restless at night. Always complaining about everything. Nothing makes her happy anymore. She misses the house where we used to live. You should hear her sometimes, how she complains. Obviously, stress.

Clara has alimony; has not completely unpacked or regrouped. Katakana has fewer diversions and a much smaller pack of admirers. The cat perhaps feels a need to say a thing or two about everything going on. That'll be seventy-five dollars, and you'll need me to come back next week and tell you the same thing. Relax. The animal interpreter always knows why your cat is upset.

It worked somehow for Tom. Basically, he loved cats, and treated them like they were the customers. The clients. And the women were the facilitators.

"Yes, yes. She is so beautiful." Tom stroked from whitish gray out to each of the blue points. He felt Katakana start to rumble in his lap. He touched her entire body, and she purred to be so examined. So manhandled.

"She doesn't always like men," Clara observed. "Not every man."

"The shoulders," Tom said.

"The shoulders?" Clara arched her own in surprise.

"Cats never carry tension in their shoulders," Tom said. "But they act out on it. Because you know they ground themselves through their heart chakra."

"She does so miss her garden. Bossing all her little friends around."

"I'm giving her a deep chakra treatment for today," Tom said, running his fingers along the spine. "You know, chakra is from the Sanskrit word for wheel." Katakana pressed her butt up into his hand and gazed back over her shoulder, her blue eyes gleaming from slits.

"This will help her energy flow and grounding, but we'll need to book another session at least."

"How many, do you think?" asked Clara, relieved

that matters were being taken into hand. "Will you take a cheque?"

And thus, Catalyst had begun to do its work.

kissing without me

"You've been kissing without me."

These words look pouty, when written, except Sebastian never pouted.

He withdrew, he turned quiet, but never pouted.

Sebastian does not accuse; he states. He observes, and then makes a statement composed of nine-tenths observation and the rest desire to share his observation. This may be a rough percentage, but leaves no room for accusation.

Sebastian just pointed things out, he stated truisms, just stated them aloud. And so he said, "You've been kissing without me," when Tom came home saturated with juniper civet, the traces of a smirk flying like a pennant over Tom's buoyant presentation. A happy shade of green. Cat hairs strewn on his sweater.

Cologne and cat hair were today's equivalent of lipstick on the collar.

Sebastian said it matter-of-factly. "You've been kissing without me." But never pouted. He just said it.

Tom felt guilt melt away, flow from him. Life in the land of stated truisms is generous and kind. He was grateful. There is an absolute freedom to sail past any concern for subtext.

"You weren't there," Tom pointed out.

He then nuzzled his face into the nape of Sebastian's neck and pulled him close. Tom relaxed his grip to look at Sebastian and then hugged him firmly, mock-growling from the fierceness of the embrace.

Tom repeated this until Sebastian came back, and then the two of them looked at each other a few silent moments.

Sebastian glanced away. "What is her name?" he asked.

Tom picked at his sweater. "Katakana. Siamese."

Sebastian shook his head. "She's Thai?"

"The cat is Siamese. Her name is Clara."

"Clara."

"The name of the problem child is Katakana."

"And you will fix the problem?"

"I hope so. The Catalyst Counselling special deep chakra massage is always a good start."

"Is she cute?"

"Yes," Tom stated, and leaned over for a kiss. "They both are."

chakra therapy

Before Katakana's chakras were completely deep-treated, Clara's chakras were also abuzz with brand new energy.

Pet therapy, in this instance, became its own treatment.

Light on therapy, but heavy on petting.

Katakana was reassuringly included in this invigoration. This quickening of life. Her input was solicited and honoured.

Sebastian's was not.

Sebastian's letter to "Brute Love"

Dear Brute,

Thank you for your column and your contribution to the world of letters.

Your reply to "Not Sure Now I Even Want to Babysit" helped me in my own life, although perhaps not the way you intended.

(Although it did not strictly apply in my circumstances, "Grow a set of balls and get on with your life" is guaranteed to become a Brute Love advice classic.)

You see, I am a man with a bisexual boyfriend. Babysitter's letter about a bisexual boyfriend's pregnant girlfriend made me think: what if my bisexual boyfriend's girlfriend became pregnant?

What would I do? I thought about it.

So then, when it happened, I was prepared.

Thanks to you, and your work.

"Grateful in Gutenberg"

Finale

Things don't just end. You can start anywhere, and go anywhere, but can't just end anywhere.

But even impermanence goes through a kind of periodic metamorphosis, as a renewal.

Even impermanence may seem like an ending, or a beginning, depending on context.

This is not meant to be a recapitulation as much as it is a reminder.

Of what is.

And how things change. And how things always stay the same. And how it may be hard to tell the difference.

Things find their way in their own time, according to Tom.

He really does say things like that, and says them like he means them too. "Things find their own way in their own time." Tom just makes this stuff up, and says it like he means it. That is his catalytic talent.

It used to be, Sebastian could not talk about things unless he had seen them. That is, he could only conceive of words to talk about objects, events, people he had actually seen (bugs!). He thought in pictures, and only found words for pictures he'd seen. Sebastian maintained a pure disinterest, a complete indifference, for ideas, or relationships, or feelings. He would not know what to do when people brought up these unseen, unknown, matters. So he would do nothing, say nothing.

He was not drawn to abstraction: his focus would dissolve.

The finale, of course, is just the last thing that ever happens.

Except, there is never the last thing. There is always happening.

Until it stops happening.

photograph by Paula Sten

George K. Ilsley is from a small town in Nova
Scotia. A graduate of Osgoode Hall, he has
biked around the Adriatic, hitchhiked to Mexico,
trekked in the Himalayas, and taught English
in Tokyo. He raised tropical fish as a boy, and
now has no pets. His first collection of short
stories, *Random Acts of Hatred*, was published
by Arsenal Pulp Press in 2003.